Books in the *Corner Park Clubhouse* series

Sophia and the Corner Park Clubhouse

**The Secret Life of Lola
(coming soon)**

Sophia and the
CORNER PARK
CLUBHOUSE

DAVINA BELL

Hardie Grant

EGMONT

Sophia and the Corner Park Clubhouse
first published in 2019 by
Hardie Grant Egmont
Ground Floor, Building 1, 658 Church Street
Richmond, Victoria 3121, Australia
www.hardiegrantegmont.com

 A catalogue record for this
book is available from the
National Library of Australia

Text copyright © 2019 Davina Bell
Design copyright © 2019 Hardie Grant Egmont

Cover illustration by Samantha Woo
Cover design by Jess Cruickshank
Typeset by Cannon Typesetting

Printed in Australia by McPherson's Printing Group,
Maryborough, Victoria.

1 3 5 7 9 10 8 6 4 2

 The paper in this book is FSC® certified.
FSC® promotes environmentally responsible,
socially beneficial and economically viable
management of the world's forests.

For Sally, of course!
Best mentor and dear friend.

And to the memory of Ms Sadlier,
who lives on in the hearts of those she taught.

CHAPTER 1

It's one of those autumn days when it's cold enough to think about marshmallows. Toasting them, I mean, or dropping them in a hot chocolate so they go all soft. (But only the pink ones, right? The best.) The leaves on my street are turning different shades of fire, and Sunnystream – the suburb where I live – looks really pretty. I'm walking through there right now if you want the full tour. I'm headed to Corner Park, where my three best friends in the entire world are waiting for me. We haven't hung out together for two whole months – not since last holidays. In other words, forever.

Belle Brodie, Lola Powell, Maisie Zhang and I (Sophia Hargraves) were best friends all through primary school – like, the *best*. But now we're in year seven, and we're all at different schools. I'm the only one who goes to Sunnystream High, and you know what? It's lonely – like, *really* lonely. Especially after what happened over the summer.

But I'm not going to think about all that today. Today is what my sister, Gracie, used to call a Full-Heart Day. You know that feeling you get on the first day of the holidays? Not the Saturday, but the first Monday, when it's ten o'clock and you'd usually be at school, but instead you're at home wearing your own clothes, maybe even your PJs, and your hair's not brushed, and you've got weeks ahead of you to do whatever you want? That's what I've got going on right now.

I'm leaving my house with two batches of cupcakes in my backpack. I baked them myself. Salted caramel, because Maisie loves everything caramel. And triple chocolate because, well, how good is chocolate?

At the end of my street, Peachtree Street, I hit the town square, which is actually more of a big grass circle. It's called Handkerchief Place and Lola has made us do like a zillion photo shoots there on her phone. It has a little white wooden gazebo in the middle that has lights strung up around it and a fountain in front, and it's super pretty. All the shops and businesses and cafes are around that square, like Sookie La La, where we get milkshakes, which is run by this nice old couple called the Greens, and Buck's, which is a grocery store, and Maisie's parents' antique store, Old Gold, which she lives behind. It's full of weird old stuff: a skeleton missing only its two front teeth, and a pirate's beard brush. In summer, people sit out here at restaurant tables, or on the warm pavement eating ice-cream from Judy's Eye-Scream. When my dad is home, we do that a lot. Or at least we used to before he left.

In fact, because I didn't have time for breakfast (major sleep-in), I think I might stop there now and get a cone and say hi to Judy. Judy doesn't treat me any differently to how she did before what happened in the summer. She just says, 'Hey kid, what up?' in that way that's half-friendly and half-professional, like you're actually just as important as an adult customer. She's only just finished being a uni student but she started the ice-cream shop all on her own, which Belle finds particularly impressive. Belle likes businesswomen who can be strong entrepreneurial role models for us. That's literally how Belle talks – I'm not even making that up.

Today, there aren't many customers at Judy's shop, and Judy looks glum. That could be because summer's ended and people won't be eating that much ice-cream for a while. Or she could be fighting with Mikie again. Mikie used to be a carpenter but now he runs the local coffee cart and he makes *really* good hot chocolate. But is hot chocolate babyish? Maybe I should start drinking real coffee, like Lola does.

Mikie and Judy are BF-GF about fifty per cent of the time and totally in love. The other fifty per cent they're fighting – really HUGE fights. That's when her ice-cream flavours have names like Death to All Boys-enberry, Man-go Away and Mikie, I'm Cherry Angry, Full of Sage. Once Mikie got a tattoo of Judy's face on his arm. She was so mad that she let the brake off his coffee cart and it rolled into Merry Creek. The power generator that runs the coffee machine got completely wrecked. I know because we helped pull it out of the creek, Belle and Lola and Maisie and I. We sort of like to be involved in what's happening around town.

Mikie is a clumsy guy, and pretty forgetful. The next week, *he* forgot to put the brake on and the cart rolled into the creek again. Often you'll find him sitting on the pavement next to his coffee cart, picking petals off a daisy and muttering 'she loves me, she loves me not'. That's when he's thinking about Judy. Lola reckons the Mikie and Judy story is better than most things on TV, which is really saying something because Lola LOVES

TV. You just never know what's going to happen next with those two.

The boy in front of me in the ice-cream queue went to Sunnystream Primary, where Gracie and my friends and I used to go. My heart sinks a little. I know what's going to happen next. When he pays Judy and turns to leave, he sees me. Looks at me. Looks uncomfortable. Looks away.

I feel my cheeks go hot. Which happens really easily when you have red hair and freckles. 'Hi Judy,' I say, trying to act like nothing just happened.

'Hey kid, what up?' says Judy like nothing just happened. (See? Told you.)

'What's your flavour of the week?' I ask.

'Vege-MIGHT-get-back-with-you-but-then-again-I-might-not,' she says. 'Vegemite and vanilla, basically. It's pretty salty. Want to try a spoon?'

'Sure,' I say, even though it sounds terrible. But here's the thing. Judy's combos always work. The Vegemite mixed with the sweet creaminess is actually total genius. 'Mmm. I'll get one of those. In a waffle cone, please.'

'Don't tell Belle about the sample spoons, OK? She'd bust my balls,' says Judy.

Belle is obsessed with getting people to stop

using plastic and creating rubbish and wrecking the environment. She's the coach of an environmental action group for primary-school kids called the Eco Warriors. Except the guy who printed their T-shirts got it wrong, so they say 'The Eco Worriers'. This is actually pretty accurate because Belle is very worried about the future health of the planet. She's the reason that no store in Sunnystream will give you a bag – not even a paper one. You'd think everyone would be used to it by now, but often people forget to bring their own and you see them with armfuls of stuff, dropping things on their toes and saying bad words. The Eco Worriers are supposed to help out by following shoppers around and picking things up.

Lots of people in Sunnystream are scared of Belle, including the shop owners. She's often described as a 'force', which I think is a code word for 'bossy but efficient'. But the weird thing is that the Eco Worriers kind of love her. In primary school, they used to follow her everywhere, like ducklings. They would ask her for advice, like what to do when their friends left them out in the playground. It was pretty cute.

'You off to the clubhouse?' Judy asks, and smiles.

Everyone in Sunnystream knows that even though technically it belongs to the local council, Corner

Park Clubhouse is sort of ours. We've played there our whole lives – after school, on weekends, during the holidays – and now that we're older, it's where we hang out. Or it used to be, before Lola and Belle moved away for school and Maisie's gymnastics got even more intense. Since the start of summer, I haven't been there either – too many memories, I guess. Without the others, it felt too sad to go there. Like eating your birthday cake alone.

But I know the clubhouse so well, it's like it lives in my heart. I can close my eyes and I'm right there, sitting on the steps of that white, wooden building – the oldest one in Sunnystream – on the edge of Corner Park oval. It used to be a cricket clubhouse – that's why it has that name. I can smell the particular smell you get when you step up onto the verandah and through the blue door, like old wood and beeswax from the polished floor and eucalyptus from the big old trees that are on one side of the building. On the other is the garden with the red Japanese maple that Gracie and I helped plant. Our dad won the tree in a raffle, but Mum wouldn't let him put it in at our house because it wasn't native to the area.

I can picture the inside of the building – the sweet little hall, about the size of two classrooms, where I've been going since Mum took me and Gracie to storytime when we were toddlers. Since then, we must have been there a million times. A zillion. It's where we've had school plays and prize nights and a town pie-eating competition, which Lola won twice. It's where we've come every year of my life to watch our local theatre group, the Sunnystream Players, put on their mid-summer murder mystery play.

In the path by the back door, there's a row of handprints from when we were in year five. We made them one night in winter when the lights of the dog park were already on, and it was so cold our fingers hurt when we took off our gloves. They'd finished digging up a drain that afternoon, so the concrete was still soft enough to stick our palms into. I'm sort of embarrassed to tell you this part because it's pretty cheesy, but when we'd finished, we all squealed and high-fived our sticky hands because it felt kind of daring, squishing a bit of ourselves into history. Like we had signed the wall in pen. By then it was dark and we'd all had to go, the concrete turning hard between our fingers, gloves in our pockets. 'Guys!' I had yelled just as everyone was heading in different directions to go back home. 'Best friends forever?'

'Literally,' said Lola.

'Obviously,' said Belle.

Through the dark, I could feel Maisie smile.

'Yeah,' she'd said. 'Forever.'

I can't wait to see those handprints again – to compare how much longer our fingers are now. 'Yup, special holiday meet-up,' I say to Judy. 'All of us.'

'You know, when I was twelve, I broke my arm climbing on the roof of that clubhouse,' Judy says proudly. 'Dislocated my elbow and everything – bent it right backwards. Best summers of my life, hanging round that place. You know the bashed-in bit on the front-right roof?'

'Sure,' I say, nodding. 'Looks like a little meteor hit it.'

'Nope – that was my sister's CD player. Know what a CD player is? I threw it up there when she told my whole class about my crush on the dad from *Finding Nemo*. Ah, good times. Say hi to the girls.'

'Nemo's dad is super nice – I totally get that. See ya, Judy,' I say, waving bye. I cross the street and head down a little no-through-road, which is where Belle lives, but not during term-time because she's at boarding school now. The park is at the end of it. As I pass by, I wonder if her mum's at home painting in their tall, skinny house. Belle will be at the clubhouse already. She's always forty-five minutes early to everything.

'Corner Park Clubhouse is never locked,' my mum always tells her clients as she drives them past. She's a real-estate agent, which means she sells houses to people. Her face is on lots of posters around town doing a really fake smile. It's kind of embarrassing. 'Not even at night. No-one in this town would ever do anything to damage it. It's the beating heart of Sunnystream. Has been for over a hundred years. That's just the kind of place Sunnystream is – a *real* community where everyone cares about each other. We're lucky like that. And if you choose to buy a house in the area, you will be, too.' Fake smile.

OMG – I wish you could try this Vegemite ice-cream. Truly, it's blowing my mind right now. Judy's Eye-Scream is just one of a zillion reasons we're lucky to live here – Mum's actually right about that. Sunnystream is a suburb on the edge of a big city, but because there's a creek on one side, and a highway on another, and Corner Park on the other, it feels like a separate little town. We even have our own town mascot, a miniature horse called Pony Soprano, who lives in a stable on Handkerchief Place and roams round the park on weekends. #blessed, as Lola would say.

Sunnystream's so safe that in primary school we could walk to each other's houses without an adult and spend the whole day by the creek. We were allowed to play by ourselves in Corner Park any time we liked. After school each day, Gracie would throw her baseball with Patrick on the oval while my friends and I would put on shows on the clubhouse stage or do handstands. Patrick was Gracie's BFF, but I haven't seen him since the summer. I try not to think about him much. Sometimes it feels like every day is just a mash of things I'm trying not to think about.

We'd stay out till it got three-quarters dark and you could hear the mosquitoes humming. When the light had faded so much that Gracie couldn't see the ball anymore, she'd come over to collect me. We'd walk home together through the twilight, our steps exactly matching, singing old songs from choir. On weekends when our parents had to work, we'd go and poke around in the clubhouse garden or help brush Pony Soprano. In the week before Christmas, there used to be Disney movies projected onto the outside back walls. Gracie and I would go early to get a spot at the front on a beanbag. I'd always fall asleep before the end. I couldn't help it – it was so warm and safe tucked up in a rug beside her.

But I didn't come here last Christmas. There are so many things I don't do anymore – ballet and Girl

Guides and swim squad. Sometimes I wonder: if Gracie were still here, would she even recognise me now?

Soph, come on, cheer up – Full-Heart Day! I remind myself. And as I get to the end of the street and see my friends across the park, sitting on the clubhouse steps, my heart really does feel full. For the first time in so long, maybe home will feel like home again. I sprint across the oval, past the stegosaurus slide. However soon I get to them, it's never soon enough. However long I spend with them, it's never long enough.

CHAPTER 2

'We're only going to be together for four hours,' Belle says, licking salted caramel icing off her fingers so she can hand out the agendas she's brought in her clipboard pocket. An agenda is a list of topics that she wants to make sure we talk about. We're sitting on the concrete steps of the clubhouse, the cupcakes spread out on the emergency picnic blanket Belle brings everywhere. There are four concrete steps leading up to the door – one for each of us to sit on, in the same place every time. Mine's second from the bottom. Belle's is at the top. 'And then I'll need to leave so I can Skype my friend Matilda,' she says. 'So let's maximise this opportunity. I'll take the notes.'

In case you can't tell, Belle has modelled herself on Hermione Granger from *Harry Potter*. She's always talking about her five-year plan and her ten-year plan and 'maximising opportunities', which I guess means making the most of things. Her family originally came from Sweden. They're descended from Vikings, which is maybe why she's tall and her hair's honey-blonde. It might also explain why Belle seems a bit fierce if you don't know her. Sometimes even if you *do* know her, actually.

'Item one,' she says as she writes in her neat, perfect cursive that could actually be a computer font. 'Breaking news: I have a boyfriend.'

'WHAT?' we say. People on the other side of the oval look over, so we must have said it loudly.

'YOU have a boyfriend?' I ask. You're probably thinking we're shocked because not many twelve-year-olds have boyfriends, but it isn't that. It's because we're surprised Belle even has time for a boyfriend. She won a scholarship to a fancy boarding school called Hollyoakes at the foot of the mountains, which surprised zero people because she's a scary genius. She only comes home in the holidays, and even though she tries to get us to group FaceTime, she does so many after-school activities that she's only ever free for twelve

14

minutes before she has to go again. Between the Row-Bots (her coding club who are programming tiny toy boats), and her campaign to get people to Say No To Straws (one of the world's biggest silent polluters), and power-studying so that she keeps getting top marks in everything, when would Belle see a boyfriend?

'Of course I do,' Belle says coolly. 'Being in a successful relationship is in my fifteen-year plan. How am I going to achieve that if I don't get any practice? To excel at anything, you need to put in at least –'

'Ten thousand hours,' we all say together, because we've heard her say this *so* many times.

Lola looks confused, maybe because she finds it hard to plan beyond lunch. And she's always been the boy-crazy one in our group, or maybe just the one who's into romance. Her whole family is obsessed with old Hollywood musicals – the ones where there's lots of swinging around lampposts and synchronised tap-dancing, and the guy is trying to get the girl, usually while sing-speaking and wearing a tuxedo. Belle refuses to watch those movies because the women don't have the chance to maximise their opportunities while the men make all the decisions. I sort of like them.

One of the things I miss about being around Lola all the time is seeing what outfit she's wearing. It's always different, always kind of bright and cool and brave, if you can call clothes brave, because she never tries to look like anyone but herself. Today it's a bright red shirt that says NERD in big white writing, a denim jacket and these puffy navy shorts that would look terrible on me, but look great on her. Her earrings are red pom-poms dangling from safety pins. I feel kind of embarrassed that I just chucked on my year six graduation hoodie that has 'Keep Calm and Graduate' across the front and three medium-sized holes in it from crawling through the back fence when my pug, Togsley, escaped last Halloween.

Lola has a dimple so deep you could stick your whole finger into it. Her parents are from Mauritius and her skin is dark and her hair is the most beautiful cloud of crazy-tight curls. Her eyes are sort of sparkly, like she's winking at you except she's not, and she is *tall* – even taller than Belle. Everyone wants to be her friend – even people who only meet her for three-and-a-half seconds. It's not just because she has great taste in fashion. Or because she makes the best earrings. It's not even because her big sister, Tally, has her own YouTube channel with almost a million subscribers. (She posts videos where she sings songs and plays the ukulele while hanging upside-down off a specially made towel rail.) It's because Lola is warm and funny and when she talks to you, you feel like you're really special. I can't remember who made it up, but we call it the Lola Effect.

Lola got in to Clives, a really famous art school, because of these big black-and-white murals she used to make. Last year she saw a guy on the news who painted giant life-like portraits on the side of those huge wheat silos in country towns. They're so real they look like photos. Lola taught herself how to do them on the side of her house, and then lots of businesses in Sunnystream asked her to put them on their walls, including the Sunnystream Post Office. Her mum was so proud, she used to always put photos of Lola's work on Instagram. But Maisie says Lola's not doing them anymore. I ditched my phone at the end of summer, so I wouldn't know. As in, I literally threw it out of my tree house. Long story. Now Lola lives on the other side of the city with her cool aunt, Claire, to be closer to Clives, and she hardly ever comes home at weekends.

'So, what's he like, this "boyfriend"?' Lola asks Belle suspiciously, taking another chocolate cupcake.

'His name's Pete. He's smart,' says Belle, 'and he plays in an improvisational jazz quartet. He's currently away hiking with his family in northern Pakistan. He was the head boy of his primary school. And he has an Instagram account just for pics of inspirational graffiti.'

Lola's eyebrows shoot up, because she loves inspirational quotes AND social media. She's obsessed with her phone. It's in her hand right now because she just Instagrammed the cupcakes.

'And he only has one eye,' Belle concludes.

'What does "improvisational" mean?' calls Maisie. I should have mentioned that since she finished her cupcake, she's been doing back-walkovers on the fence rail. Maisie never sits still unless she's coding, and she can even do that while she's balancing on something.

'Improvisational means making stuff up,' says Lola. 'What do you mean one eye? Like, he lost it or he never had it? Isn't that weird?'

'One eye isn't weird. Like that kid in *Wonder*,' I say. *Wonder* was our favourite book in year five, and if you haven't read it, you seriously should.

'He never had it,' Belle says briskly. 'And honestly, you don't notice it after two seconds because he's a dream. Any other questions, or shall we get back to the agenda?'

I have heaps of questions – like, so many. What's it like to have a boyfriend? How do you know when somebody wants to go out with you, or if they're just being nice or friendly or whatever?

'Have you kissed yet?' calls Maisie, who is always after details.

'Once, closed lips. No spit, no tongue, no regrets,' Belle says. 'Right, item two on our agenda. Maisie, get over here. Next up is the Kumon Issue.'

Maisie cartwheels over, then sits down and hugs her knees, tucking her face into them. That's a classic Maisie pose. She's not shy at all but you might think that at first because she hates any kind of attention. Gracie would have said that's ironic, because Maisie is a gymnast and when she competes, the entire stadium stops to stare. She's in Team Future, which is the serious squad for gymnasts from all around Australia. She trains twenty-two hours a week, before school and after, too. When I see her do gym, I get the same feeling as when I look up at the stars in the countryside. Like you can't believe something could ever be so perfect – it makes your heart hurt a little and your throat get tight, it's that beautiful.

Maisie is my BFF and in case you can't tell, I am SUPER proud of her. At primary school, if we had to choose partners, it was me and Maisie together, and Belle and Lola, who love each other, but kind of drive each other nuts and couldn't be more different. Maisie still lives in Sunnystream, behind her parents' antique shop, but she goes to school in Cloud Town, which is the next suburb over. Her parents chose it because of the music program and how well the kids do academically. She's in about seventy-seven string quartets, which is pretty funny because she's actually tone deaf, and I'm not saying that to be mean. I'm saying it as someone who has played a lot of SingStar with her. She's trying to learn the drums so she can switch to the big brass band, but it's hard to fit in anything else around all her gym.

At the end of the last holidays, her parents told her that she couldn't train on Wednesdays anymore because it was clashing with Kumon. Kumon is this special after-school maths program that's supposed to make you into a child genius who becomes a dentist. Maisie says it just makes her want to cry. Her parents don't want her to quit gymnastics if it makes her happy, but they also care a lot about schoolwork because neither of them got the chance to go to uni. They told my mum about it at the Don't Panic It's Organic stand at the school fair last year.

'Well, my parents say I have to do Kumon Plus on Wednesdays again this term,' says Maisie. 'But Coach

Sanders said that if I miss Wednesday practice, I won't get to train with Coach Jack.'

We all make the kind of sounds that say 'oh no', because we know what that means. Coach Jack is the best coach in our district. He was Gracie's coach, too, before she got obsessed with baseball and quit gym. Coach Jack actually reckons Maisie could get to the Olympics one day, but right now the next step is going from Level 9 to Level 10. That's a huge deal, because there are only ten levels. After that it's the Nationals. Maisie says Coach Jack makes her believe she can do anything – that maybe she really could get to the Olympics. But Lola is more interested in his man bun. 'Long hair is so hot,' she sighs whenever we bring him up.

'No Coach Jack, no Olympics,' says Belle briskly. 'Well, we're just not going to let that happen. How are your grades going?'

Maisie isn't dumb. When she says she is, it really hurts my heart – like, I can actually feel it. She just isn't a total genius at schoolwork like her big sister, April, who is totally on track to be a dentist. And her other big sister, June, who is currently at Junior Astronaut Camp in the Florida Keys.

'Umm,' Maisie says, rubbing her eyes with her palms.

For the zillionth time I wonder how she can even stay awake at school. To get to training she has to catch two buses, and the second one doesn't even leave from the place where the first one stops. She has to run across a shopping centre car park in the dark. But Maisie isn't scared of anything. And she's REALLY good at not getting caught doing anything bad. Belle always says Maisie would make a good assassin, which is someone who kills people in a silent, sneaky way. That's why one of her nicknames is Killer.

'Well, my marks aren't … great,' says Maisie.

'It must be hard to maximise study windows when you're training all the time,' says Belle. 'My new friend Matilda's a rower so I totally get that. She has to get up at four in the morning too.'

'Horrifying,' says Lola, who can sleep till noon, easy. She takes a selfie wearing Maisie's cat-ears beanie.

'Can you put that thing away?' asks Belle.

'Sorry, guys. Just putting this on Snaps. Gotta –'

'Keep the streak going,' we say, because we've heard her say it ten million times before.

'Well, you're giving off vibes that you don't even care about the Kumon Issue,' says Belle.

'Sorry,' says Lola, taking a quick picture of Belle looking grumpy. In about three seconds, she's made her eyes super big, with purple devil horns sprouting out of her head.

Maisie giggles. Belle glares. I try not to laugh because when Belle's in a bad mood, everyone is in a bad mood. You know those people?

'Seriously, guys. We only get to be together for such a small amount of time now. We can't waste it on screens,' she says. 'Maybe we should take Soph's lead and all get rid of our phones.'

There's an awkward pause and I can feel my face go hot again. I didn't ditch my phone to, like, make a protest or lead a better life or make a stand against technology or anything. I did it to avoid talking to my dad. I did it so I wouldn't have to talk to him after he left to live in the city and he called every night, over and over, and I never picked up because I was too mad at him to talk. And sometimes, when my mum's old laptop is being super slow and FaceTime goes all wonky, I really regret it, too. I want to say all that, but it's harder, these days, to say what's in my heart. I just turn red and swallow, wishing things were different.

But then Lola winks at me, just at me, and I get a fizzy feeling, like maybe I'm not the worst human after all. The Lola Effect, I guess. 'Stop being so bossy,' she says to Belle.

Belle rolls her eyes. Lola rolls hers back.

'Maisie, I've got some openings in my schedule these holidays,' says Belle. 'I could tutor you in maths – get you ahead enough to ace this term. I help Matilda all the time. She was homeschooled so she's a little behind everyone else.'

'Can you shut up about Matilda for two seconds?' asks Lola. 'Mais, what if you could practise gym somewhere else? Our basement's pretty big. We could move Rishi's drum kit. He wouldn't mind.'

And he actually wouldn't. Rishi is Lola's big brother and he's the kindest person I know. He's in year nine and he's teaching Maisie to play the drums. I could talk about him forever but I'll shut up now.

'Aw. That's so nice,' says Maisie, reaching for the cupcakes. 'But I need equipment. The beam and all that. Are any of these red velvet, Soph? I love that cream-cheese icing that you … Oh.' Maisie's voice trails off because Lola and Belle are giving her death stares. Making red velvet cupcakes is something else I don't do anymore.

'Well, let's park this issue for now,' says Belle, which I think means 'talk about something else'. 'Item three: Sunnystream news. Do you know, since I've been gone someone's torn down all the Say No To Straws posters?'

Belle says, outraged. 'And have the Eco Worriers printed out any more? No. Sometimes I wonder what they do with their time.'

'Well, most of them are only eight,' says Lola, pulling a strawberry Chupa Chup out of her bag. 'I'm guessing they're still making up horse games and all that stuff.'

I miss making up games. I miss primary school and using skipping ropes to pretend we were horses-and-carriages. I miss Maisie teaching us gym tricks at lunch and walking on our hands around the library when Mrs Whiffin wasn't looking – all the way from the front desk to the non-fiction section and back. I wonder if the others miss those things too, but it's probably just me. I guess I haven't really told you anything about myself, have I? I'm not really sure what to say because so much stuff in my life is different now. I wonder which part of me is still me.

But here are some things that are still the same. Apparently I have really big eyes, but big compared to what? I like to bake. I like to read. I love my friends. I'm the only one of us at Sunnystream High, the local school, and I hate it. I have a pug called Togsley and a GIANT rabbit, as big as a human baby, called Lemon Tart – well, I sort of do. She lives with Maisie at the moment. She'll let you dress her up in anything you can think of.

'Let's brainstorm how to strengthen their community spirit and re-ignite the fire of social justice,' says Belle.

'That sounds boring,' Lola says. (At least I think she does – the lollipop makes it hard to tell.)

Belle ignores her. 'Just because I'm gone, doesn't mean I'm gone, if you get what I mean. Sunnystream needs –'

'Defenders of the future,' we say together, because we've heard her say it a squillion times before.

'Exactly. What's happened around here? When was the last time Sunnystream held the annual Corner Park Hot Sausage Dog race?' she says. 'Or Slip N Slide Sundays?'

We all pause. She's right. We didn't even have one Slip N Slide Sunday last year. We didn't do that in February, or have our Ape-ril Fools Photo, where the whole town crams onto the clubhouse verandah in monkey masks for a big photo that Mr Stavrianou, who runs the local paper, takes with his old film camera. We didn't have Lettuce Be Married in June, either, which is where married people can come and renew their wedding vows in the vegetable patch of the clubhouse garden.

We turn to each other, realising at exactly the same time what's going down in Sunnystream. And it isn't good.

CHAPTER 3

'Mayor Magnus,' we say. Belle glowers so much, her eyebrows practically join together.

Have you heard about this guy? He's loud and rude and rich, and somehow last year he became the mayor of Sunnystream, though all the parents say they didn't vote for him. Maybe he hypnotised them. Because before he was the mayor, he was a hypnotist who wore a purple sparkly cape. He made about a zillion dollars travelling around hypnotising people at shopping malls, and then he started building his own shopping centres. He called himself Sparky Mark but he's changed that now to Mega Mayor, and he still wears the cape. Since he's been in charge, he only cares about his #biggerisbetter! campaign, and so our Sunnystream traditions have started disappearing, little bit by little bit. Maybe that's the reason it doesn't feel as much like home anymore. Or one of the reasons, anyway.

'Well, we're going to do something about it,' Belle says briskly.

'Like drop a giant glitter bomb on his office,' says Lola.

Belle glares at her with a 'you're not taking this seriously' face.

'But we only have the holidays,' Maisie points out. 'That's just two weeks.'

'A lot can happen in two weeks. We'll schedule a separate meeting to discuss. Moving on to item four: One sentence of family gossip. I'll go first. Francine is still dating Punk Sherman.'

'No WAY!' we say. Francine is Belle's mum. Punk Sherman is her latest boyfriend – the forty-fifth since Belle's dad left when she was three. Belle hates Punk Sherman, but then, she hates all her mum's boyfriends. Punk Sherman has buck teeth and says he is a circus engineer. Belle thinks that's just a cover story because he doesn't have a job. Who on earth is a circus engineer? Sunnystream doesn't even have a circus.

The other news is …

Lola: Her big brother, Rishi, and his band just got their first song on the radio. (Amazing!)

Maisie: Someone actually bought the pair of stuffed mongooses (mongeese?) from the antiques shop, which means we can't use them as extras when we make our music videos anymore.

Me: My dad is still living in the city apartment.

'Well, you never know, Soph. Maybe he's actually just – hey, who are *those* guys?' Lola asks, pointing towards the park, and from how interested she sounds, I bet one of them has a man bun. Or, at the very least, some kind of ponytail.

I turn to see four men in fluoro orange vests walking towards us. They stop by the clubhouse fence and one of them pulls a roll of orange tape from his pocket. He takes a while to find the end of the tape and I can tell Lola is about to offer to do it for him (she has really long nails) but then he finds it and wraps it around the fence rail.

Maisie and I look at each other like 'what the heck?'.

'Hi, I'm Lola,' says Lola at the exact same time as Belle says, 'Sir. What exactly are you doing?'

The old guy who's just arrived looks a bit like Santa Claus except with an Akubra hat, and it seems like he's in charge because he has a clipboard and a pen.

'Top of the morning,' he says to us, tipping his hat. 'Just filling out the paperwork. This grand old dame is getting pulled down soon.' He waves his arm at the clubhouse, and the garden, and even the fence.

'WHAT!?!' we all say together.

Holy SMOKE.

'Shocked' does not even begin to describe this feeling. It's like finding out someone is going to lasso the moon and drag it right out of the sky, and I have to blink hard so I don't cry. Maisie crosses her arms and I think there might be tears in the corners of her eyes, too.

'But the clubhouse is ours!' says Lola, scrambling to her feet. 'You can't do that!'

'Well, it's not technically *ours*,' says Belle, who likes us to be accurate. 'But it *is* the beating heart of Sunnystream. Haven't you read *Sunnystream: A History*?' she asks Aussie Santa as she stands up too and puts her hands on her hips, which is called a power pose. 'Without the clubhouse, we wouldn't have a town. Back in 1897 –'

'Just following orders here,' he says. He sounds kind but also firm, like there's no point in arguing with him. 'I'm Steve Morrison, by the way. I'm the town's building inspector.'

'Isobelle Brodie,' Belle says, stepping forward to shake his hand. I see him wince a little as she grabs it, just like our old primary-school principal used to when Belle won awards, which was practically every week. 'A powerful handshake shows a powerful mind,' she always says. I've practised with her before and literally felt the bones of my hand crunch together.

'Doesn't look much like the beating heart of anything,' calls one of the guys with the tape, which is all the way around the fence now. The other guys snigger. HEY! I want to say, all fired up. It feels like he's insulting my grandma or something.

But then we turn around to look at the clubhouse, and it's like we're seeing it for the first time, or with different eyes, or something like that. The white paint is peeling off the wood. The bright blue door is hanging off its hinge. A couple of the windows are cracked and one doesn't even have glass in it. Looking through it we can see that the place is chock-a-block with random bits of furniture. The stairs where we ate the cupcakes are crumbling on the sides and one has a huge crack running across the middle that looks sort of like a freaky evil clown mouth.

'Whoa. This is a real dump,' Maisie says with wonder in her voice. 'When did it get like this? Weren't we just here for something recently? Oh …' Her voice trails off as she remembers the thing I am always trying to forget. It was the start of summer, four months ago. Almost exactly.

'Maybe we didn't notice then,' Lola says gently, looking over at me. 'Maybe we were thinking about other things and it wasn't quite as bad.'

'You can't do this without informing the public,' Belle says to Mr Morrison. 'The residents of Sunnystream have a right to know.'

'We've told them,' says Mr Morrison sadly. 'Put a notice up at Handkerchief Place, and it's on the council website, too. But nobody's seemed too fussed so far. It's such a shame, because the building's filled with junk, sure, but it's still –'

'What do you mean *junk*?' Belle asks sharply. 'What is all that stuff?'

'A while ago, the mayor sent over everything that was in the council building's basement so it could be stored here instead. All kinds of old things. It's free to a good home now. You girls can have first pick if you like. If you can lift it, you can take it. Then I'll get someone to clear the rest out before the building gets bulldozed.'

BULLDOZED! It seems so brutal, imagining our

sweet Corner Park Clubhouse being ripped apart and flattened. It makes my tummy hurt to think about it. 'But why?' I say. I want to yell, but it only comes out as a whisper.

Mr Morrison frowns. 'Mayor Magnus says there's no money to do the repairs. But you know, there's actually nothing wrong with this place,' he says. 'I mean, structurally. Apart from that broken door and a few new bits of glass, it just needs a lick of paint, new steps, and a bit of spit and polish.' He pauses and looks up at the row of little windows above the door. They each have different coloured panes – yellow and orange and pink. 'I got married here, in fact, the winter that the roof of the church blew in. And the thing about this place,' he adds, 'is the acoustics.'

'We're getting a little off topic here,' says Belle. 'About the bulldozing. When –'

'The acoustics are phenomenal,' Mr Morrison says a little dreamily. 'My barber-shop quartet actually recorded an album here, back in the day.'

'Which day?' Maisie asks curiously. I would describe Maisie as a very curious person.

'The 1960s,' says Mr Morrison. 'Those were different times.'

'Was your band good?' asks Lola. 'Like, famous?'

Belle clicks her tongue. 'I think we should probably go back to discussing –'

'I don't mean to brag,' interrupts Mr Morrison, 'but people did say we were the Beatles of Sunnystream. Yes siree, we had some good times at this clubhouse.'

'So did we,' I say, remembering our year two ballet concert here, when we were dressed as red robins in *The Magic Faraway Tree* and I accidentally fell off the stage. I think of Girl Guides and afternoon tea after Dad's cricket matches and the end-of-season picnics for Gracie's baseball team, the Comets. I remember listening from backstage when Belle won her big public-speaking competition with a speech about how good the world would be if we could educate girls in poor countries. That's how she got to do her TED Talk. (You should google it – it's pretty inspiring.) I remember singing Christmas carols by candlelight the year it rained and we had to hold them inside. How cosy it felt with the sound of the rain on the tin roof and everyone's faces glowing and Gracie singing the harmony for *Silent Night* next to me. I think about the red Japanese maple and the handprints out by the back door and my parents coming here to sit on the steps at the end of their wedding night when my mum had taken off her high heels. Gracie used to love that story.

She would always get Mum to tell it on long car rides. I think of Maisie doing flips on the fence rail – how she gets braver every year. How we've all grown up here, little by little, and got braver in our own ways. 'Can't you do something?' I swallow. 'Please?'

He looks at me like he really is sorry, but shakes his head. I start to feel panicky, like I'm trying to breathe through cotton wool.

'That's progress for you,' Mr Morrison says, clipping his pen to his clipboard. 'I guess we don't need the clubhouse now we've got the Shark Tank. All the community groups meet there now – storytime and oldies' yoga. And nobody's come by to work in the garden for weeks.'

The Shark Tank is a giant new nine-storey building on the other side of Sunnystream, next to the highway. Mayor Magnus has his offices there, on the top floor. It was built SUPER quickly, and it just opened last year. My mum tells her clients the Shark Tank is a 'multi-media entertainment complex'. It has the local library and a cinema and a huge theatre with red velvet seats. I guess that's where the Sunnystream Players put on their shows now. It has a Japanese pancake parlour (Ja-Pancake Par-LA!) with an awesome ping-pong table. When it first got built, my dad vowed never to take us there. But the Japanese pancakes have this really delicious wasabi mayonnaise. Now, though, I sort of regret ever going. The building's named after Mayor Magnus, whose nickname is The Shark because he's big and scary. He thinks that's a compliment, which tells you a lot about the kind of guy Mayor Magnus is.

'But that's not the same!' Lola says. '*This* is where all our memories are.'

Lola is right – every tiny bit of this clubhouse holds a memory. Not just of Gracie, but of the times we were all together here, Belle and Lola and Maisie and I. Thinking about losing it makes me feel as if I'm about to be swamped by a giant wave, like in the disaster movies that Gracie loved but that I couldn't watch before bed because of bad dreams.

'Well, we're heading to the Shark Tank this second,' says Belle, bristling, 'to see what Mayor Magnus has to say for himself.'

'We are?' asks Maisie. 'Oh yeah – I guess we are. But what if he tries to hypnotise us?'

'We'll kick him,' says Lola fiercely. 'Right in the n–'

'Bye, Mr Morrison,' says Belle.

'Be careful,' Mr Morrison warns us. 'That Mayor Magnus is a big old bully. You watch out.'

CHAPTER 4

'Do you guys have holiday homework?' asks Lola. I recognise her 'nervous but trying not to be nervous' voice, and I bet she's trying to distract us from what we're about to do. We're walking to the Shark Tank with our arms around each other, four in a row. You might think that sounds awkward, but Maisie's really good at jumping over sprinklers and ducking around trees and dog leads while the rest of us stick to the footpath. Maisie's the kind of person you want to run a three-legged race with – she's got great reflexes.

Lola looks across at me and winks, and when I smile back, I feel myself relax a little. 'I seriously can't believe how much homework year sevens get,' she continues.

'It's torture.'

'Are you kidding?' says Belle. 'We get literally none. I have to make up my own to keep my mind sharp. I trade it with Pete. My boyfriend. And Matilda. Obviously. What about you, Soph? What's it like at Sunnystream High?'

'Some,' I say, feeling myself blush. 'Sometimes.' The truth is, I haven't done any all term. And none of the teachers have even asked me about it. I feel suddenly embarrassed, like I haven't been maximising my opportunities.

'We have so much I could spew,' says Maisie. 'Seriously, you have *grown*,' she tells Lola. Maisie's a shrimp, so her arm hardly reaches around Lola's shoulders now.

'Seriously, you have *not*, little Killer,' Lola says to Maisie, and strokes her hair.

'My friend Matilda is pretty tall,' says Belle. 'We went apple picking and she didn't even need a ladder. Did you know that apples are actually part of the rose family? It's a fascinating –'

'Who's Matilda again?' says Lola sharply. 'I thought you said you had a boyfriend, but are you sure you're not actually in love with *her*?'

'Matilda's my best friend from school,' says Belle.

'She is *super* smart. Even though she grew up on a pistachio farm and didn't go to school till she came to Hollyoakes.'

'Apples, pistachios. Sounds like you're making this stuff up,' says Lola.

'I'm not! One of her mums is a famous actress. You've probably seen her on your stupid phone.' Belle says the famous mum's name and she is actually *super* famous. Heaps more famous, even, than Tally.

'I might be going to the pistachio farm,' Belle says happily. 'Next holidays.'

I feel my stomach scrunch up and my throat go all tight, like I might cry. And it's not just because of what Belle just said about missing the holidays. It's also because I haven't made any new friends this year – not one. At lunch I just walk around so that I don't have to sit alone. People do the weird looking-at-me-and-then-looking-away thing, or they whisper as I go past. I feel like a pale, freckly, red-headed ghost, floating around and making people awkward, like a dad wearing underpants outside of his jeans. In class, I don't say anything. I sit on the sides of the classroom, hoping I fade into the walls.

Thinking about it makes me so ashamed that tears spring up in my eyes. What kind of loser doesn't make a single friend – not even someone in the lunchtime Monopoly club? Luckily coz of how we're walking, I don't think the others notice the tiny tears. I haven't told anyone, not even Maisie, how lonely I am at school. I need these holidays. I need my friends around me, like they always used to be.

As we get to the big revolving doors at the bottom of the building, I swallow and wipe my eyes. *Full-Heart Day!* I remind myself crossly, and join in taking turns to run through the doors, over and over. It sounds stupid but it's actually a great way to burn off our fear till we're ready to step into the lobby.

'Remember when –' Lola glances at me and stops. I know she's remembering taking turns pushing Gracie's wheelchair through the sprinklers at our year six graduation party but she doesn't want to say. 'Never mind. Where's the elevator?'

From the top floor of the Shark Tank, you can see the whole town. As we walk from the lifts, I look out the window, wondering if I can see my mum driving her clients around, frantically pointing out all of Sunnystream's great features. We come to a huge pair of glass doors. We all hesitate because they look so official. Also, I'm kind of scared of the hypnotising part. But Belle isn't.

'Ma'am!' the secretary cries as Belle marches in and then goes straight past her shiny metal desk. Everything in this building is shiny and grey or shiny and gold. 'Young lady! Do you have an appointment?'

I feel like I'm going to throw up, but Belle just turns and glares, and her eyebrows do the joining-together thing. Weirdly, the secretary sits back down and waves her through, like she knows her. *Has Belle been here before?* I wonder. Maybe this is where she dropped off the petition for her Say No To Straws campaign last year.

We follow her straight through the giant gold door and into the mayor's office. I feel half terrified and half proud. Saving the clubhouse means saving part of our town's history, and that will affect all kinds of people – not just us. But especially us. It might even bring the whole town back together.

Everything in here is so gold, it's blinding – everything except the giant fish tank that takes up an entire wall. Mayor Magnus is sitting at his giant shiny gold desk with his deputy, Bart Strabonsky. He's like Mayor Magnus's sidekick – like how Batman's sidekick is Robin. I suddenly remember that at Mayor Magnus's hypnotism shows Bart Strabonsky used to be dressed as a cowboy. Partway through the shows, Mayor Magnus used to pretend to saw Bart Strabonsky in half. Bart Strabonsky also has a monocle. Do you know what that is? Like glasses but for only one eye. It's like something from a cartoon. Lola says Bart's creepy, but Belle thinks that's judging on appearances, which is an immature way to approach personal relationships. For the record, I also think he's creepy, but mainly because it's creepy how much he sucks up to Mayor Magnus.

Mayor Magnus and Bart Strabonsky are playing cards. To be more accurate, they're playing Snap. This doesn't surprise me because, well, everyone in Sunnystream knows Mayor Magnus isn't that smart. At least once in every single conversation he says, 'Kaboom!' Even when he opened the new wing of Sunny Heights, the nursing home, he said, 'Kaboom!' My mum thought it was very inappropriate but Gracie loved it. If she were here now, she wouldn't be trembling. Gracie was always so brave.

Mayor Magnus is tall and his shoulders are SUPER wide. He reminds me of Miss Trunchbull from *Matilda*. But a man. With fluffy honey-blond hair. And a cap that says MEGA MAYOR. Oh, and he has his purple sparkly cape on. 'Hey fans!' he says, looking up for half a second before he yells, 'SNAP!' and giggles.

'Looks like you guys are busy with important work,' says Belle, crossing her arms and glowering at Mayor Magnus.

I don't think Mayor Magnus gets sarcasm, though, because he says, 'You bet!' which was also his campaign slogan, alongside #biggerisbetter!

'You know what you need to do?' he says to Belle, like he's going to offer her some deep and profound advice. 'Girly, you gotta take that frown and turn it upside down.'

'"Girly" is a very outdated word and quite disrespectful,' says Lola. 'We're young women.'

'What's this about?' says Bart Strabonsky, not looking up from the cards. 'You're wasting the mayor's precious time.'

Belle looks like she's about to explode.

So I follow my friends' lead and screw up all my courage and jump in. 'Is it true you're bulldozing Corner Park Clubhouse?'

'That dump? Of course. Should have done it years ago,' says Mayor Magnus. 'That place is way too small. It's big things that will make Sunnystream great again.'

'That clubhouse is dangerous,' says Bart Strabonsky smoothly. 'It's ugly. It needs to go. Like a puppy that needs to be shot.'

'In the head,' adds Mayor Magnus, and he actually giggles.

'WHAT?' we all say together.

'You know,' says Mayor Magnus, 'an old puppy. A sick one. Putting it to sleep. It's the nice thing to do. You bet!'

'Puppies are never old,' I say. I know pretty much everything about puppies because of Togsley. 'And you don't put dogs to sleep by shooting them.'

'Besides, what about the history?' says Belle.

'Of puppies?' asks Mayor Magnus.

'Of the clubhouse!' says Belle. She pulls from her bag *Sunnystream: A History*. Does she carry that book everywhere?! 'That clubhouse has been the site of many important moments in Sunnystream's history. Completed in 1903 in the style of –'

Mayor Magnus closes his eyes, tilts his head back and acts like he's snoring. Then he cracks himself up and Bart Strabonsky does this really fake nose laugh, like he thinks he's on TV.

We all look at each other like, 'VOMIT!' These two are the literal worst.

'I'm going to knock down that dirty little dog kennel and build a giant apartment block there called … "The Muscle Tower",' Magnus says, turning towards his giant fish tank. 'I'll put an aquarium in the lobby that's five storeys tall. I'll put a shark in it that's as big as a submarine. Then I'll put a submarine in there too, and I'll drive it around. Might even give you a ride.' He winks at Belle in this really goofy way.

URGH. Mayor Magnus is every bit as awful as everyone says. Truly, all he cares about is himself, and he doesn't give a rat's tail about all the things that he's destroying.

Hot anger starts bubbling up in my chest. I dig my nails into my hands so hard that I know they'll be making dark little half-moon dents in my palms. Why does everything I love keep getting taken away?

'The Muscle Tower is a *fantastic* name,' says Lola like she totally doesn't mean it.

'Thanks, doll face,' Mayor Magnus says. 'Thought of it all by myself. And when I've finished with the clubhouse, I've got big plans for the whole park. Kaboom!'

'You can't get rid of the park,' Maisie says calmly. 'Everyone would go crazy. Where would anyone play sport? Or walk their dogs? And what about Pony Soprano? It's where he runs around.'

'That horse is too small to be the mascot of this town,' complains Mayor Magnus. 'We should have a rhino.' He picks up his phone to record a voice memo. 'BUY RHINO,' he yells into the microphone.

Do you know who would be finding this pretty funny right now? Gracie Hargraves. Do you know who isn't? Me.

Bart Strabonsky leans towards us and narrows his eyes. 'Between you and me, I think Pony Soprano is going to have a very sad accident someday soon. You just wait.'

'OMG,' says Lola.

'Is that a *threat*?' says Belle.

'You're so evil,' says Maisie.

'Nobody would ever hurt Pony Soprano, you oaf,' I say – except it comes out more as a squeaky yelp because I'm shaking with rage. 'And nobody is going to buy your stupid apartments, either.'

Maisie puts her hand on my arm to calm me down.

'No-one can hurt a rhino,' says Mayor Magnus. 'And when people hear about the Muscle Tower, they'll give me a big pile of money to invest – you'll see. They forgot about that clubhouse the day I opened the Shark Tank and started serving those dee-licious Japanese pancakes. Even the Sunnystream Knit-Wits don't meet there anymore.'

Maisie and Lola turn to each other and roll their eyes, but you know what? I think he's right. People *do* like new shiny things. The Knit-Wits are a knitting group who are all, like, eighty. Gracie used to follow them on Instagram, and they'd always post selfies from the lobby of the Shark Tank, where they were using the free wi-fi. Are we the only ones who still care about the clubhouse? My anger feels like it's melting into a puddle of despair.

'You're nothing but a giant buffoon,' says Belle, looking him straight in the eye. Her nostrils are flaring like Pony Soprano's, she's so mad. 'People respect honesty. And fairness. And intelligence. And people helping each other out. They'd never give their money to a pumpkin-head like you.'

'One week!' says Mayor Magnus, pushing the tips of his fingers together. 'In one week … KABOOM! The clubhouse will be gone.'

'So you won't touch it for a week?' says Belle. 'Till next Monday? You promise?'

Mayor Magnus nods enthusiastically. 'I'm gonna ride there on a bulldozer myself, next Monday at 10 o'clock. Do I have a bulldozer?' he asks Bart Strabonsky. 'GET BULLDOZER!' he yells into his phone.

'Well, you'll probably want a big crowd to come and

watch you,' says Belle smoothly. 'We can arrange that.'

(Huh?!)

Mayor Magnus literally licks his lips. He adores a crowd. I wonder if he'll wear the purple sparkly cape then too. 'Thanks, doll face. Appreciate.'

We turn to go and he calls, 'Hey, girlies, want to look at my tropical fish? Biggest collection in the southern hemisphere, right here. Stay and pull up a chair. We can play cards.'

'Are you crazy?' asks Belle. 'I'd rather be eaten by an actual shark, limb by limb with my flesh being ripped apart –' (um, whoa – intense) '– than spend one more *second* of my life with you.' She marches out and the others follow her, but when I look back, I swear Mayor Magnus looks like he's about to cry. For real. When he sees me watching him, he glares so fiercely that his eyebrows practically cross.

'Whoa. Did anyone else see –' I begin.

'Are you crazy?!' Maisie asks Belle as she punches the buttons on the lift. 'Why did you offer to bring him a crowd?'

I've been wondering the same thing, actually. I couldn't bear to stand there and watch the clubhouse be torn apart. Honestly, it would be like seeing Pony Soprano being shot, or someone blowing up Gracie's bedroom. Even thinking about it makes my breathing go tight and shallow.

'Do you need your asthma puffer?' Maisie asks.

I shake my head. I want to explain that thinking about losing the clubhouse makes me feel as if I'm suffocating – like my heart is actually breaking – but I don't have the words.

'I think she's just freaking out a little,' says Lola. 'Deep breaths, Soph. Like this.' I copy her until I feel a bit calmer.

'Do you think we're going to sit back and let that moron crush the best thing about this place?' asks Belle. 'We're going to organise a giant rally to stop him. With the whole of Sunnystream. Next Monday at 10 o'clock.'

'A rally like in tennis?' Maisie asks, confused.

'That's the other sort of rally. I mean like a big protest,' says Belle. 'With speeches and people holding signs and yelling things. This could be bigger than Say No To Straws!'

'We could chain ourselves to the bulldozer!' says Lola. 'To stop Mayor Magnus tearing it down. And then we can film it. That would totally go viral.'

'Nobody's chaining themselves to anything,' says Belle as the lift reaches the ground floor. 'I'm talking about intelligent political action, not some stupid internet thing. Seriously, guys, we might be the only ones who can make a difference to that clubhouse. We can rekindle the Sunnystream spirit. So let's do it. Are you in?'

The lift goes 'ping!' and the doors open and as we step out, I feel that prickle of electricity you get when someone has a good idea. Thinking Fire, Gracie used to call it. The others feel it too – I can tell by how we're suddenly grinning at each other.

'I'm in,' says Lola quickly.

'I'm in,' I say quietly.

'I'm in,' says Maisie, 'but I can't talk about it right now coz I've got conditioning in forty-five minutes.' Conditioning is like strength classes. That's how Maisie can lift a giant tractor tyre above her head. I saw her do it on year six camp. 'What about tomorrow? Planning meeting?'

'Yes, but not before ten,' says Lola firmly. 'Holiday sleep-in.'

'Eight,' says Belle firmly. 'I'm Skyping Matilda at one and Pete at three.'

'Nine at the clubhouse,' I say, because I like to keep the peace.

'We won't be able to sit inside because of all the junk,' Belle points out, 'and it's supposed to storm tomorrow.' Belle is a very diligent observer of weather patterns.

'My basement?' says Lola. 'But apologies in advance for my annoying family.'

'I love your family,' I say, because it's true. The Powells' house is the opposite of mine now – it's loud and busy and chaotic. When they stop squabbling, the whole family can sing in the most amazing harmonies. You should hear them do Christmas carols – it's like *The Sound of Music*. Their basement is a giant games room with a ping-pong table and a disco ball.

'Deal,' says Maisie.

We race each other out the revolving doors and into the autumn sunshine. Lola's first and Belle is last, and we do a group hug before we go our separate ways. Our arms, locked tight, feel super strong. *Together, we are stronger.* That was the quote we all chose to put under our photos in the Sunnystream Primary yearbook. When I'm with these guys, it feels like we can do anything.

CHAPTER 5

If you've ever been woken by a miniature pony landing on your bed, you'd know what it feels like to have Maisie Zhang drop through your window before sunrise, straight onto your covers.

'Pony Soprano?' I croak into my pillow. 'Is that you?'

Maisie crawls in next to me and lies there for about three seconds, which is how long she can sit still at any one time. Since the summer, she stops by sometimes on her way to training. She climbs up the tree house and then along the ridge of the roofline. There's a little window in the roof that I always leave open for her. My mum says it's called a dormer window and it increases the value of our house significantly. I can feel the chilly morning air on her clothes, the cold metal of the studs on her jeans against my legs, but I don't move away because if I close my eyes a little, it feels like I'm sharing a bed with Gracie.

I dreamed about Gracie again last night. I dreamed she was at the clubhouse, running through the garden. I dreamed that she ducked and weaved around the sundial that Lola decorated in a thousand tiny mosaic tiles, and the little wooden lending library that Belle built after watching a YouTube tutorial. I dreamed that she shimmied up the red Japanese maple, and then she disappeared.

'Can I plait your hair?' Maisie asks.

'Sure,' I say dopily, and drag myself up to sitting as she flicks herself around onto my pillow. 'But you'll have to get the knots out first. What's the time?'

'Ten to five. Sorry.'

'No matter,' I say. I stayed up super late making cheesecake and then I couldn't get to sleep – not for ages – because I was thinking about the clubhouse, half worried, half excited, half scared. (Is that three halves?) I got up at four to bring Togsley into my room. Sometimes the sound of his snoring makes me feel better. But Maisie wasn't to know.

'Soph?' she says, just when I'm dozing off again. 'Do you think I'm dumb?'

'Don't even say that,' I say, suddenly wide awake. 'It hurts my feelings.' And it truly does. 'No dumb person could do gym like you.'

'Yeah, but that's just sports.'

'What about coding? And drums? And –'

'OK, shut up now,' says Maisie, but not in a mean way. She's one of those people who hates it when people say nice things about her. You know the type?

We're quiet for a while. With real friends, silence is never uncomfortable. That's something I read on Lola's Instagram once and I think it's super true. Sometimes I miss Lola's Instagram posts, but there's no way Mum will buy me another phone now.

'There's a new move I'm trying at gym,' Maisie says eventually as she finishes de-tangling and separates my hair into sections. 'It's really hard. I think about it all the time. I see it on my eyelids – on the insides,' she says. 'Does that even make sense?'

'Is it a vault?' I ask. Maisie's best apparatus is the vault because she's so short and strong. In gymnastics, the four apparatuses are the vault, bars, beam and floor. Maisie finds floor routines the hardest because when she's concentrating on her moves, she forgets she also has to wave her arms around a lot like she's a Spanish bullfighter and/or someone from *Romeo and Juliet*, which is what's supposed to make the audience fall in love with you and also get you a perfect ten.

'No,' Maisie yawns. 'It's on the beam. Back handspring, back handspring, backflip. But I need to practise it more. Maybe I should be doing double training these holidays. Maybe … maybe I don't have time to be part of this whole saving-the-clubhouse thing.'

'You do!' I say, turning round to face her so quickly that the plait falls out. 'Whoops – sorry. We need you, Maisie. Please? You can practise in the clubhouse when it's finished. It'll be like your own private gym.' I've been looking forward to the holidays for so long that I can't bear to think about us not spending them all together.

'Maybe,' says Maisie. She sighs. 'I should go.'

'Stay!' I say, and wrestle her, trying to pin her hands down. Early-morning wrestling is one thing my dad is the actual best at. But Maisie is a natural because she's pretty much all muscles. In three seconds she's flipped me over and is sitting on my back. I'm laughing, but I can't breathe that well so it comes out like a seal coughing.

'Victory!' Maisie yells, forgetting to be quiet and sneaky so my mum doesn't know she's here. Mum is sort of obsessed with kids getting enough sleep. She would *not* be OK with a five o'clock wake-up.

Downstairs I hear her feet land on the floor next to her bed.

'Go!' I hiss. 'See you later, at the Powells'. And be safe,' I whisper after her as I close the window. But I don't need to say that. Maisie never, ever falls.

Just as I'm climbing back into bed, there's a tap on the window and Maisie sticks her head in again. 'Hey, remember when I climbed up the drainpipe at the clubhouse and water-bombed Belle's Harry Potter book club?' She grins. 'I really do want to save it. I'll make the time.'

That's a weird fact about Maisie: she hates Harry Potter. The books, the movies, all of it. She thinks he was too mopey and not grateful enough for his incredible powers. Do you know who loved Harry Potter? Gracie Hargraves. She read all the books out loud to me with a zillion different voices for all the characters. Her idea of heaven was something she called a Reading Party, which we set up under my dad's desk. Blankets, snacks, the whole works.

I feel tears start to slide down my face as Gracie slips

into my mind. I'm sick of this wishing feeling, because I know that wishing can't ever bring her back. I'm sick of being sad, and of people being so weird around me. I'm sick of feeling like a freak at school – of walking around and around at lunchtime, nowhere to go, no-one to sit with. These holidays were supposed to be a break from all that. But it's not going to be the same as it used to be because nothing is the same anymore.

Gracie was always the one who organised the holidays when we were left home alone by ourselves, and the nights after school when our parents were working late. She pretended she was a cruise-ship director, wrote menus, wrote the scripts for our plays, volunteered us to help out at Sunnystream Animal Shelter. She made everything into something you'd want to remember, like it was an important event.

You're probably thinking, 'Oh, she must really miss Gracie.' But that isn't enough – it's so much bigger than missing, this feeling in my chest. I didn't know how to describe it, but then Lola emailed me a quote she found on the internet, and truly? It helped more than anything anyone said. It went like this: 'To describe how I miss you isn't possible. It would be like blue trying to describe the ocean.' And that's exactly how it is. I don't just miss Gracie. I *am* the missing. Like the ocean is blue. It's as if I've turned into something entirely different – a whole other creature, like a mermaid. And part of the missing is missing the old me. I thought the old me would be at the clubhouse, waiting. But now there might not be a clubhouse, and I don't know how many more things I can lose.

When I get up an hour later and pad down the stairs, Mum is just about to leave for work, even though she got in so late last night that I didn't see her before I went to bed. I want to tell her about the clubhouse, but she's whipping around the room in that crazy 'I'm forty seconds behind schedule' frenzy, shoving things into her briefcase and aggressively curling up her phone-charger cord into perfect coils, all exactly the same length. 'Oh – money for dinner tonight,' she says as she hears me coming, riffling through her handbag. 'I meant to leave some on the table. Here you … Oh.'

She looks up and sees that I've been crying. I can feel that there's snot crusted on my face, which has that salty puffiness. You know that feeling when you cry so much your skin kind of aches? I've got that now.

'Sophia, what's wrong?' Mum asks. But she uses a voice that I know so well. It's the one where she feels as if she should stay and talk about something emotional, but she's actually got to get to work and doesn't really know how to deal with it anyway. It was always Dad who did the 'come here and tell me all about it and I'll always love you anyway' thing.

'You can go,' I say, my voice kind of squeaky from all the crying. 'I know you probably have to be somewhere.'

'I would stay, sweetheart, it's just that I'm showing a couple that converted bungalow over on Tea Cake.'

Converted bungalows are a type of house that's worth a lot of money, especially the ones on Tea Cake Crescent. I know because Mum used to point them out to me and Gracie all the time when she was driving us places, like my ballet classes over in Cloud Town and Gracie's away games for baseball.

'See that, girls? Lovely houses,' she would say, 'with wonderful proportions.'

'Like the girls on *America's Next Top Model*,' Gracie would say.

'You're not really watching that trash, are you?' Mum would ask disapprovingly. She thinks reality TV is the devil.

'Not watching it. Just auditioning for it. Aren't we, Soph?' That would literally be my mum's worst nightmare.

'Grace Hargraves, your attitude is bordering on obnoxious.'

'Oh, it's way beyond that,' Gracie would say. She had such a cheeky wink.

'Seriously, go,' I tell Mum, trying to sound more together. 'I'm fine.'

'Well, if you're sure, here's fifty dollars. Or you can get some Uber Eats. Do you still have the app on your phone? That charges straight to my card.'

'I don't have a phone anymore,' I remind her for the millionth time, taking her guilt money.

She looks at me hesitantly. 'Sophia, your father and I –'

'LA LA LA LA LA,' I say, covering my ears, closing my eyes.

When I open them again, she looks even more uncomfortable. 'It's Tuesday, so tonight after work I'm –'

'At a networking evening,' I finish. As far as I can work out, that's when Mum's real-estate friends sit around and talk about real estate. 'See you tomorrow then. Maybe. Whenever. It's not like I don't have keys.'

I remember when Gracie and I had to stand on a box to reach the lock. We've always had keys. 'Such independent children,' Mum would say. 'Or neglected,' Dad would say. 'Either way, we must be doing something right.' He was proud of us – even when we weren't winning things or getting on teams, which Gracie usually was.

'A big heart is more impressive than a big trophy cabinet,' he'd whisper when we were sitting together, watching her walk up on stage at the clubhouse to get yet another award. Dad is basically the opposite of Mayor Magnus. Everyone in Sunnystream knows him and loves him. He has these springy curls that jump out from his head, like electricity, and kind blue eyes, the type that crinkle up at the corners.

But he's not here. He hasn't been since the Christmas holidays, when he moved to the city apartment. I haven't spoken to him since then – that's why I threw my phone out of the tree house. When he calls the landline, I run up to my bedroom and stuff a corner of my doona into my mouth.

Before Gracie got sick, he used to travel a lot for work. He's a TV writer and he used to go back and forth to Los Angeles. You'd think I wouldn't notice the difference between him being in LA or in the city. But as the front door closes and I put sourdough bread in the toaster, wiping my snotty face, for the zillionth time I can feel it – his not-here-ness. Hovering over the house like an actual thing – like a drone that follows me from room to room.

'Pickle,' he had said the night before he left. 'Want me to put oil on the flying fox before I go?'

'Don't call me that,' I snapped. 'And I don't want you to do anything.' I looked up from the cookie dough I was kneading at the kitchen bench. 'Except stay. Please? Dad, *please*. Don't go.'

He sighed. He pulled up a stool and put his head in one hand and watched me. He watched as the dough came together in a ball and I rolled it out, carefully sprinkling flour on the rolling pin so it wouldn't stick. He watched as I cut out the biscuits with the rim of a glass, like Grandma Jean had showed me, and laid them on the trays. I didn't mess up a single one.

'Soph,' he said, picking up a dough scrap, 'you can visit me in the city. Any time. It won't be forever. It's just that ... Mum and I, we've been through a tough time. We need some space, apart, to –'

'YOU'VE been through a tough time?' I said, slamming the oven door shut, and my voice was kind of all over the place. 'You think this has been tough for YOU?'

I thought of the day Gracie came back from the hospital after her second treatment, all hot and crying. I'd gone to stroke her head, just how she liked it, and a bit of her hair had fallen out in my hand. It was so springy and beautiful, that hair. It was the most Gracie thing about Gracie.

'You'll look good bald,' I'd told her. 'Like a rock star.'

'I'm going to save a bit,' she'd said. 'Will you keep it? To remember me?'

'It will grow back,' I'd said.

'I don't think so,' said Gracie.

I thought of how her rabbit, Lemon Tart, sat on her lap when she had to start using the wheelchair, so patient, and then how she tucked herself into the crook of Gracie's elbow all those months when she was stuck in bed. I thought of how hard it was to see Gracie be sick. How it was even harder to watch her be brave.

'Don't think I'll ever speak to you again,' I told Dad as I set the oven timer for the cookies. 'Maybe *I'm* the one who needs some space.'

'I'm so sorry,' he said softly.

But I didn't say anything back.

CHAPTER 6

'Hi Mrs P,' I say when Lola's mum opens the door of their giant house at nine o'clock. The sky's grey and it looks like it might storm. The wind is whipping the falling leaves around, like we're inside a snow dome. Lucky I didn't have far to come because I live over the Powells' back fence.

'Sophia! So lovely to see you. You look nice, baby! You're here for the meeting about the clubhouse?' says Mrs Powell, pulling me in for a hug that crunches my bones. 'You girls, always doing these good things round town. When are you coming round to watch some more old movies, hmm? We have so many now on the Netflix.' She kisses me on the cheek and then bustles back to the kitchen. Even though she's the strictest mum I know, Mrs P is *so* nice.

Don't judge, OK, but for once, I have made a real effort with my appearance. I'm wearing a denim skirt and a stripey top and Gracie's peach lip gloss. I've tried to put my hair in a bun on top of my head. I feel half grown-up and half like a little kid pretending to be grown-up. We're meeting in Lola's basement, which is huge, by the way, and it's where Rishi's band practises. They're called RexRoy and everyone in Sunnystream is crazy for them. The lead singer is called Grey Dare and a guy called Jules plays the electric banjo and designs all their posters. Lola has a crush on him like you wouldn't believe. 'Banjos are *incredibly* hot,' she says. But are they really?

So, umm, Rishi is the reason for the lip gloss etc. As I walk down the stairs, the cheesecake I made last night banging against my leg in its bag, I see him sitting at the drums, showing Maisie something. ARGH! I can feel myself going red already.

I almost trip on the bottom step as he looks my way and says, 'Hey, Hargraves.' Hargraves is my last name. I think I told you that already. I don't know because when I'm around Rishi I can't remember what my name is or anything important. When he smiles, I get the tummy love feeling.

'Hey Rishi,' I say, trying to do a casual wave that turns out like a robot kid putting their hand up in robot school.

'Your turn, Killer,' he says to Maisie, jumping up off his drum stool so she can sit down.

Even though it's stupid, I feel jealous when he calls her Killer. I feel jealous as I sit down on one of the big couches and he hands her the drumsticks and then snatches them away at the last second and they laugh together, like it's a joke they've had going for ages. His laugh is higher than you'd think for someone so tall. Did I mention he's tall? Everyone in their family is – even the little sisters, Gwynnie and Pop. It's nice. He's nice.

'How's the ukulele going?' he asks me.

'Oh – ah, I haven't played it since … since forever,' I say, feeing myself blush even more.

Rishi nods like he understands. As Maisie starts drumming, he looks at me. His eyes are the same as Lola's, sparkly brown and usually cheeky, but right now they're serious. 'I read a book last week that I think you'd like,' he says. 'It's about a girl who reminded me of you. Let me go find it. That's sounding good,' he calls to Maisie, 'but a little lighter on the snare.'

As Rishi disappears up the stairs, Maisie sticks her tongue out at me and crosses her eyes. That's her 'you were talking to a boy' face.

'Shut up, Killer,' I say, trying not to smile.

Maisie isn't that fussed by boys. Maisie never seems that fussed by anything, except gym. 'Chill' is how everyone describes her.

She stops drumming for a second. 'I probably shouldn't stay for the whole thing,' she says, and makes an 'eek sorry but I have to be strong' face. It's the same face she made when she had to leave my Mexican-themed birthday party before pin-the-tail-on-the-taco.

I try not to take it personally, but sometimes it's hard. I'm so proud of Maisie, but sometimes it hurts that I know I'll never come first. It'll always be gymnastics over me.

Belle arrives with all her brainstorming notebooks and Maisie gets out her iPad. Lola comes in and says hi and sits down, all while typing stuff on her phone and eating two pickles, which is actually a skill. Today she's wearing tights that have this pattern of brightly coloured diamonds – pink and black and yellow and turquoise – with black basketball shoes and an aqua-blue blazer with the sleeves pushed up. Her earrings are tiny peace signs.

It feels so familiar, having them all close around me. I know my friends like I know my bed, or Togsley, or the feel of my hairbrush running through my hair. I wish every day could be like today, us together, no school, the autumn leaves in Corner Park starting to fall like giant amber snowflakes. You know that feeling? Like you miss something even while it's happening, and you know you'll remember it forever.

'OK, get off Ultimate Pizza Fantasy now,' says Belle to Lola, kind of breaking my whole remembering-the-good-times vibe.

'I am NOT playing Ultimate Pizza Fantasy,' says Lola, flashing her screen at us. There's a video of two really cute baby orangutans putting their hands over each other's eyes. 'I'm making people aware of Orangutan Outreach so that –'

'Whatever. If you're here, actually be here,' Belle says sharply. 'If you're just sitting there scrolling, you might as well leave. *Time is how you spend your love* – you put that on your Instagram yesterday. So spend it on actual people, you giant poo emoji.'

'YOU'RE the poo emoji,' Lola says back, grinning.

'Phone addiction is an actual thing,' says Belle, and

I can tell she's about to go on a serious rant. 'My friend Matilda did a presentation about it. She found out that app companies have researched the exact colour combinations that our brains will respond to with –'

'I'm sure it was fascinating,' says Lola. 'Almost as interesting as *Sunnystream: A History*. Have you lent her that yet?'

'Guys,' says Maisie. 'Seriously?'

Belle's eyes are flashing and now Lola is sticking out her chin and I don't want them to fight but I can't think of anything to say besides, 'I made cheesecake.'

And suddenly everything's OK again.

'YES!' they all say together. 'Soph food!'

'I'll get the plates,' says Lola, and sprints up the stairs two at a time.

'OK,' says Belle as I get it out of the container. 'Down to business. Item one. How are we going to convince people to come to a rally to save a clubhouse that nobody cares about anymore?'

Then there's a *really* awkward silence. We look at each other and swallow a lot.

This plan seemed so exciting yesterday! But even though we're almost thirteen and – I don't mean to brag here – pretty mature, we're actually just kids, and Mayor Magnus is the actual mayor. Plus he's obsessed with getting his own way. He wears people down until they just give up, which is how my mum thinks he got elected. The only way we can stop him is if we convince the ENTIRE town to stand up to him.

'I know that the news about the clubhouse has been on the internet,' I say, 'so I guess some people know about it, but maybe … maybe we need to remind them *exactly* why the clubhouse is so special. Why it matters to *them*. And to all of us. And why old things can still be good things. And how buildings hold the memories of times we've loved. And the people we've loved, too.'

The others turn to look at me, sort of surprised. I guess it's the longest thing I've said in a while.

'But it's looking pretty crummy,' says Maisie. 'Shouldn't we, like, fix it up a bit before we try to get everyone feeling so emotional about it? It's hard to care about a dump. It'd be like trying to get people to care about that car park out the back of Buck's where the dudes from Sunnystream High skate on the dumpsters.'

'Where exactly?' asks Lola, returning with plates and those things that are half spoons and half forks. Sporks. And a giant knife, which she hands to me. Lola thinks skating is super hot.

Belle just ignores her. 'You're right,' she says to

Maisie. 'Plus, it'll be harder to demolish it if it's looking all sweet and smart. And while we're getting it back in working order, we can arrange the rally. We'll need stuff for repairs.' She starts listing supplies. 'Paint. Rollers. Cement.'

'I can deal with paint,' says Lola, 'but who has a clue what to do with cement?'

'And, um, where are we getting the money for all of that?' asks Maisie. Maisie is really good at saving money. I, on the other hand, am not. 'Mayor Magnus sure isn't paying.'

'As if that guy would ever pay for anything,' Belle spits. Truly, she hates him with the fire of a squillion suns – maybe more. 'We'll have to fundraise.'

'But how?' Lola asks as I slice into the cheesecake.

'We could grow our hair really long and shave our heads and sell our hair?' suggests Maisie.

'In one week?' says Lola sceptically.

'You can put tonic on your hair to make it grow faster,' Maisie says. 'I saw it on TV.'

'Since when are you ever allowed to watch TV?' Belle asks.

Maisie grins. 'I have my ways.'

'LOLA!' Tally yells from upstairs. 'What have you done with my –'

'NOTHING!' Lola screams back, not even waiting to hear what Tally's looking for. 'And stop accusing me of stealing your stuff!'

'Then stop stealing it!' yells Tally. 'You little thief!'

'MUM!' yells Lola. 'Tally called me a THIEF.'

'Tally, Lola – kitchen! NOW!' calls Mrs Powell.

Lola rolls her eyes. 'Sorry,' she says. 'This will just take a second.'

It actually takes quite a few seconds and quite a bit of yelling to sort out the situation.

'Should we leave?' whispers Maisie.

'No – this is fascinating!' says Belle, who is an only child. 'Do you think she's going to get grounded again?' Lola gets grounded a *lot*.

But not this time. 'Sorted,' she says as she slides back down the bannister. 'Sorry, guys. Where were we? Still on the fundraising ideas?'

'We could put on a concert to raise money,' I say, thinking back to last year's Sunny Stream of Talent Show. Belle's mum played 'Shake It Off' on the panpipes and it went for a really long time. Maisie's dad put on a leotard and a headband and pretended to be an aerobics instructor, and our school principal, Mr Jenkins, laughed until he literally cried. Maisie's dad is really funny.

Then my mum was supposed to sing 'Edelweiss' in a duet with me. Gracie learned it on the guitar and everything so she could play along. She practised SO hard, but at the last minute Mum couldn't come because she was working. I pretended I didn't mind about 'Edelweiss', but I really, *really* did.

'Nah. Forget it,' I say. 'Stupid idea.'

'There are no stupid ideas,' Belle reminds me as Gwynnie and Pop come barrelling into the room and start jumping on the sofa. They are super cute – they're only, like, four and six – but boy, they are cheeky.

'Can we play?' asks Gwynnie, the older one, climbing onto Belle's lap.

'It's not a game,' says Lola, and I can tell she's trying to be patient. 'This is grown-up stuff. Why don't you go upstairs and see what Tally is doing?'

'Tally told us to leave her alone and come down here,' says Gwynnie.

'Did she now,' says Lola darkly.

'Can I have cake?' asks Pop.

'No,' says Lola. 'You're allergic to dairy and this is a cheesecake.'

'It doesn't look like cheese,' says Gwynnie. 'Are you lying again?' She turns to us, looking kind of smug, and says, 'Lola lied to Mum and Dad about school and she got into heaps of trouble. She said that she'd been –'

'OK, show's over,' says Lola, jumping up and throwing one kid over each shoulder.

The girls scream, and Pop reaches out and grabs a fistful of cheesecake on their way past the coffee table. She mashes it into Lola's hair and across one eye. Lola shrieks and drops her, sort of maybe a little bit on her head, and Pop begins to wail. Boy is she *shrill*. I'm starting to remember why we never usually hang out here. Stressful! Rishi rushes in to see if there's been some catastrophic accident, and then Gwynnie starts to cry too, but I think it's just to get his attention. Then there's a giant crack of thunder as the storm outside finally breaks, and Gwynnie and Pop start crying for real.

'What do you think Lola lied about?' Belle whispers to me as Mrs Powell swoops down the stairs to sort things out. 'That sounded kind of interesting.'

'I heard that,' Lola calls. 'Busybody.'

'Magnolia!' says Mrs Powell. 'Baby, that is no way to talk to a friend. What's happened to you lately? So sulky.'

'Nothing,' snaps Lola. 'Can everyone who's related to me please respect our privacy and leave the basement NOW?'

'We'll talk about this later,' says Mrs Powell firmly as she herds everyone away.

Lola clears her throat, looking embarrassed. 'Yes, well, apologies about that. Where were we?'

But right then Rishi comes back down the stairs and hands me a book with a purple cover. 'Here you go, Big H,' he says. 'And, um, sorry, guys, but I need to kick you out now. We have band practice here in ten minutes.'

'But we're right in the middle of our meeting!' says Lola. 'That's not fair!'

'I'm sorry,' says Rishi, 'but we're writing our new album. It's important.'

'And so's the clubhouse!' Lola fumes.

'I know, I know.' He really does sound sorry. He really is the nicest guy on earth. Maybe even in the whole galaxy. 'Did you guys know that RexRoy used to jam in the clubhouse after Seniors Bingo on Tuesdays?' he tells us. 'Our first gig was there – back when we were a One Direction cover band. No way they can tear that place down. Don't you usually meet over there anyway?'

'But we were going to make nachos!' says Lola.

'It's OK,' I say, and Maisie nods.

'We need to check out what needs doing at the clubhouse, anyway, to formulate a more accurate forward plan,' says Belle, starting to whisk all her paperwork back into her backpack.

'Thanks for the book,' I say to Rishi as we're leaving. 'You look great. Oh! I mean, *it* looks great. The book, I mean. Not you. Oh! I mean, you too. But not … Bye, Rishi.'

As I sprint up the stairs, my face literally on fire, I can feel Maisie grinning beside me.

'Shut up!' I whisper.

'Didn't say anything,' she whispers back.

CHAPTER 7

Once we're at the clubhouse, we realise it's in worse shape than we could have imagined. It's actually almost impossible to get in there because of all the junk, but even from the doorway we can see how grimy everything is. There are giant loops of ceiling cobwebs, which Lola thinks look like epic chandeliers, and the walls are the colour of old teeth.

'Don't lose heart,' says Belle after we've squeezed past all the stuff in the entrance and looked over the rest of the clubhouse. 'Basically, it's just a lot of clearing and cleaning and painting and fixing. We can just google that stuff and watch online tutorials. Easy. All we need is a five-step plan.'

And so together we make this one:

Step 1: Clearing Out (the junk)

Step 2: Cleaning Up (and fixing)

Step 3: Operation Undercoat (that's the first bit of paint)

Step 4: Paint Paint Paint (no explanation needed)

Step 5: Finishing Touches (to make it seem professional)

We decide to get cracking on Step 1 after lunch because, not counting today, we've only got five days to do everything. Oh – and we have no money. And no plan of how to get any. And we also need to plan the rally and get the whole of Sunnystream on our side. That sounds doable, right? Sort of …?

'By the end of the week it's going to look incredible,' says Belle confidently.

'Um, a question … Are we actually allowed to be doing this?' I ask. 'Are we going to get in trouble?' I actually *really* hate getting into trouble.

'Of course we're allowed,' Belle says quickly. 'We're saving history from an evil pony-killing, puppy-slaying shark. What's wrong with that?'

I'm not entirely sure that's how the law works. But when I think about it, I'm pretty sure my mum would think it was a good idea if she'd stop and listen for three seconds. She loves community action. Or the idea of it, anyway. So I guess it's OK.

'OMG – once we've fixed it, we can decorate!' says Lola. 'Just how we want! Like, we'll get to choose the colour and the vibe and –'

Just as I start to say 'Yellow' and Maisie starts to say 'Purple' and Lola starts to say 'Boho loft', Belle starts to say, 'Sounds expensive.'

The rain's cleared up, so thankfully we can work outside, because all the dust was starting to give me asthma. We write lists of jobs and supplies and responsibilities. We look up prices online and plan trips to the Hard Hair Store, the two-in-one hardware store and hairdresser in Cloud Town. That's the suburb next to ours, and it's sort of our rival, but mostly in a jokey way.

By lunchtime, everything's sorted except the cash. We are seriously pumped and my heart is definitely full. It's like last term never happened and we've seen each other every day forever. It's like their friendship's wrapped around me, bright and warm, like a lasso made of light. Standing on the verandah, we all look at each other and smile, and I know they feel it too.

'I think it's time for an inspirational quote,' says Belle.

'Oh brother,' says Maisie.

'Hit me,' says Lola.

'*Kites rise highest against the wind, not with it.*' She pauses. 'Lots of people think that's by former British prime minister Winston Churchill but it's actually not. Interestingly, lots of his quotes aren't actually –'

'The point?' asks Lola.

'What we're trying to do might not be easy. We might fail. We might be publicly humiliated in front of hundreds of people,' Belle says, and now she's really getting into Public-Speaking Mode. 'The place we cherish most in the world might be *ripped* from our hearts before our very eyes. We might –'

'Sorry, didn't you say this was going to be inspirational?' demands Maisie. 'This is just a downer.'

Belle stops. She shrugs. And then she grins and yells, 'Stacks on!' and tackles us to the ground in a big bunch, which is pretty wild and irresponsible in Belle's world.

It's warm at the bottom of the pile of our limbs. I can smell Maisie's apple shampoo – the same one I used at her place when we were little enough to have baths together. Lola's ribs are right up against my ear and I can hear her heartbeat, strong and bold, just like her.

'I can't breathe,' I say eventually, laughing.

'I know CPR,' says Belle. 'I've read about it. We'll

rescue you. We won't let you down.'

'I know,' I say, as everyone climbs off me. 'I've always known.'

'So exactly when are we going to get to the decorating part?' Lola asks. Lola and I are the first ones back from the break we just took to get lunch at home and change into work clothes. We're taking Togsley for a quick spin around the park while we wait for the others to come back.

I'm excited about the decorating bit too. Mum's never let me decorate my own room properly – at least, she never let me make every single choice. Once she let me and Gracie choose the paint colour, but then she said that meant she could decide on the bedspreads, and she chose really boring grey ones.

'Well, I guess first we need to get the money together. And remember we have to do the cleaning and the fixing first. Hey – cool! You changed your earrings.' She's switched the peace signs for four tiny cut-out paper dolls holding hands. 'How did you get them so small?'

Lola shrugs like it's no big deal, but when she's

proud of herself she tries not to smile in a way that makes her dimple poke into her cheek, so I can tell. 'All for one and one for all,' she says.

Then neither of us says anything for a while. Sometimes, even though I've known her forever, I get a little intimidated by Lola. Lots of times over the years I've felt like I was too uncool to be her friend, and if she thought about it for three seconds, she'd realise that too, and go hang out with Maggie Mair instead. Maggie Mair makes her own movies, even though she's only thirteen. One of them got shown at a short-film festival in America. The festival was on the edge of the desert and she actually got to go there. She made a short film about *that*, which was basically her skipping through sand dunes in bare feet and a denim pinafore. Maggie Mair is beautiful, too, in a blonde skateboarder way. She has so many followers on social that she is practically breaking the internet.

'I like your overalls,' I say to Lola. It's probably a stupid thing to say. What I actually want to ask her is why she stopped doing those big murals, but I don't quite know how.

'They're just Tally's old ones,' she says. 'For dirty work.'

'Oh. Right. Of course. I knew that.' I cringe and

change the subject. 'Togsley is happy you guys are back. He's missed you.'

'Good old Togs,' says Lola. 'Smartest pooch on the planet. Remember when we did that online doggy IQ test?'

'He is pretty smart,' I say proudly. Togsley can actually ride a skateboard. Probably better than Maggie Mair. 'Not as smart as Lemon Tart, though.' It's true. For a giant (actually giant) rabbit, Lemon Tart is basically Einstein. She would be great at Kumon.

'I haven't seen her for ages!' Lola says. 'Since, like – oh. Sorry, Soph. I didn't mean to ...' She trails off, like she wants to finish the sentence but she can't.

'It's OK,' I say.

'Are *you* OK?' she says. She stops and I stop and she turns to me.

I don't know what to tell her. I haven't talked about any of this stuff with her. Or with anyone. It's all just sitting in my throat, pressing down, making my jaw ache – my head too, some days.

'I mean really, though,' she presses. 'You're so quiet these days. I feel like I want to be there for you but I don't know how.'

I shake my head. Lola grabs my cheeks and presses our foreheads together.

'I carry your heart,' she whispers. 'Got it?'

I nod. I get it. 'I carry your heart' is from a poem that we really love. Our year four teacher, Ms Sadlier, helped us memorise it. She said it was originally written from a guy to a girl, but it could also just be to someone – anyone – who made you feel like you had fireflies inside you. Ms Sadlier taught us a new poem every fortnight. Truly, she was the best teacher we ever had.

'But seriously,' says Lola as we start walking again, 'have you had any more ideas about the money? I wondered about making earrings to sell, but they take so long and we don't have enough time. Then I thought about stealing Tally's stuff and selling it to all her lame internet fans, but she'd probably murder me. I asked Rishi if he'd put on a fundraising concert, but RexRoy still haven't written all the songs for the new album and he thinks doing a live show will mess with their creative process. And that's all I've got.'

'Those are all great ideas,' I say, impressed. 'All I thought of was a photobooth where you can take selfies with Lemon Tart dressed in different costumes. Do you think anyone would pay for that?'

'Maybe,' says Lola loyally, but I can tell she doesn't really mean it. And to be honest ... I don't think any of this is going to happen. We just don't have long enough to get the money together. We're going to lose Corner Park Clubhouse, and Sunnystream won't ever be the same again.

Lola and Togsley and I walk along in gloomy silence until we hear someone dinging a bike bell. In the distance, we spy Belle cycling across the oval. A giant sandy-coloured Labradoodle, tied to her handlebars by his leash, is running along beside her.

'Sergeant!' we yell and run to meet him, scruffling his ears. I let Togs off the lead and he and Sergeant sniff each other like they're old pals. Sergeant belongs to Mr and Mrs Green, the old couple who run Sookie La La. We've known him since he was just a little puppy in a basket in the corner of the cafe, when he smelled like toast and smiled like one of those clown machines at a fair. Sometimes, in return for free milkshakes, we'd walk him for Mr Green. He was so little he'd get tired walking even halfway around Corner Park and we'd have to take turns carrying him like a baby. Now he's huge but he still has that same crazy smile and he bounds like his feet are too big for him, which they sort of still are. He's the actual best.

'So good to see you!' Lola says, kissing his neck. 'What are you doing here, buddy?'

'Mr Green is paying me to walk him,' says Belle.

'So that's some extra cash for the clubhouse.'

'That's a good idea,' I say, marvelling for the squillionth time at how smart Belle is. 'Better than any of the ones we've had so far.'

When we get back to the clubhouse, Maisie's there to greet us, running backwards along the fence rail, and I am secretly super happy that she hasn't gone to training. 'Sergeant!' she cries, and does a front somersault dismount so she can run and pat him. They end up wrestling together on the ground, rolling over and over. Togsley looks at me disapprovingly, like he's saying 'look at those goons', and then trots into the clubhouse garden. 'Hey – come back!' I call. But he ignores me and runs over to sniff at the trunk of the red Japanese maple. I can feel everyone turn to look at me as my eyes fill up with tears.

Last Christmas Eve, I wheeled Gracie over here. It was the last time she ever left the house. She didn't feel well, said she couldn't see properly, but she still wanted to come. Mum didn't think she should but Dad squeezed Mum's hand and said, 'Let her go.' The sun had only just gone down so the sky was hazy and orange and bright. Stringy bits of eucalyptus bark crackled under her wheelchair as we crossed the park. The kids had done their nativity play here earlier, so there were bits of hay all over the ground. Pony Soprano had been the donkey that Mary had ridden on – he does it every year. He's got great dramatic timing. 'Text Patrick,' Gracie croaked as we came through the gate. Patrick was Gracie's best friend. He was the kind of kid who always had a zillion things in his pockets: coins, a USB, a key ring with a laser on it, a mouse called Cheeks. He always had a pocketknife, and that's what Gracie wanted. I wheeled her over to the red Japanese maple – right up to the trunk. You're not meant to cut things into trees – it's sort of bad, like graffiti – but I don't think anyone minded what Gracie carved. It's a love heart, big and lopsided. Inside the heart there's writing – uneven, like the person who did it couldn't see very well. But you can still read it. It says, 'Gracie was here.'

'It's not just a clubhouse,' says Belle gently, as we stand there watching Togsley. 'We get that, Soph.'

'Don't worry about the money,' Lola adds. 'We'll think of something.'

I don't say anything – the words get stuck in my throat. But my heart yells THANK YOU. I just hope they can hear it.

We get going on Step 1: Clearing Out. The dust over everything gives me asthma twice. Luckily I always have my inhaler in my pocket. We drag the stuff out onto the grass – all the old mashed-up costumes and some mismatched armchairs and a cricket bat and three broken kettles and half the head of a giant sphinx, and a lot of office stuff from the council building that Mayor Magnus must have had moved here, including two filing cabinets that Belle thinks might contain top-secret documents. Also thirteen old mops and a lot of actual rubbish.

But some of it's really heavy, like a bed with a marble frame, and a giant Converse sneaker that's also a sofa, and a fan the size of an aeroplane engine. Even Maisie can't lift the sneaker.

'We need to call every strong man we know,' Lola says.

'Or woman,' says Belle. 'Let's be inclusive. But seriously, how do we get rid of this stuff?'

'We could pay someone to take it away, I guess, but that seems stupid when we're trying to make money.' I shrug.

'So … light bulb! People pay *us* to take it away!' says Lola. 'I'm putting this on Insta: GARAGE SALE

TODAY. Rare one-off pieces of furniture! Yours if you can lift them.'

This is total genius, and Maisie and I quickly try to arrange everything on the grass so it looks like a garage sale and not a rubbish pile. Within fifteen minutes, people are showing up.

Rishi's band arrives and ends up taking the Converse sofa to put in the Powells' basement. Miss Claudine comes over from Cloud Town and nabs the marble bed for her ballet studio. Rishi and the band boys help load it onto Mikie's truck so he can drive it there for her. I hope Judy doesn't get jealous. Punk Sherman shows up and takes all the mops. 'Great collection you've got here,' he says, sounding impressed. Belle looks pained and goes off to Skype her boyfriend. I sneakily follow and listen in, and I kid you not, they spend most of the convo counting backwards from one hundred to one in Mandarin to try to keep their brains sharp. It's not really what I imagined dating to be.

By four o'clock, all the stuff is gone except for a baby grand piano with a hole through the middle. We have enough money for the cement to fix the steps, plus a bit left over! It's only a tiny thing, but it feels big.

By four-thirty, Belle has booked a rubbish and recycling dumpster. Turns out the guy who delivers it restores pianos so he takes the baby grand in return for a major discount. (Who knew bins cost so much? There goes the leftover money.)

By five-thirty, we're sitting on the grass outside the clubhouse, so tired we can't even talk. Even Maisie looks exhausted. And now that it's empty, it's easy to see just how much we still have to do. The walls are that weird crusty brown. Lots of the floorboards are broken. There's a layer of grime on the floor that you can make patterns in with your finger, it's that thick. I've loved Corner Park Clubhouse since I was born, but right now it is kind of gross, and who's going to care about saving a dump? This is going to be way harder than I realised. I can tell the others are thinking the same thing: is it stupid to think that a bunch of kids can do anything?

'Think about Malala,' says Belle. 'Think about Anne Frank and that boy who became a doctor when he was nine – not the one on TV, the actual real-life one. And see you tomorrow morning at seven.'

Nobody says anything. We don't have the energy to think about Malala. We don't even have the energy for goodbyes. One day down, four to go, and we're still basically broke. Can we really make this happen?

CHAPTER 8

On the second day of saving the clubhouse, aka Step 2: Cleaning Up, I park my scooter outside the clubhouse alongside Belle's bike, which is already locked against a tap. It's only five to seven, but the others are already sitting on their steps. I can't help smiling when I see them there. Just like old times. Maisie has Sergeant on her lap and Lola has a really pretty Dalmatian on hers. I wish I'd brought Togsley, but I didn't want him to get in the way.

'Who's this?' I ask.

'That's Clover,' Belle replies. 'She's beautiful but very stupid. No offence, Clover. Did you get today's updated to-do list on your email?' she asks.

Lola rolls her eyes. 'Yes, everyone got your zillion emails. And before you ask, no, I haven't had any more ideas about the money.'

'Me neither,' I add sadly. Unless you count my daydream about paying to kiss Rishi at a kissing booth, but I'm not going to share that.

'Me three-ther,' says Maisie.

'Well, we've still got until tomorrow to pay for the paint and stuff, I guess,' says Belle, 'so let's get going on the inside cleaning. We need to clean before we can paint. And that floor grime is disgusting.'

'Should we walk Sergeant first? And Clover too? Who does she belong to?' I ask, stroking her silky black ears. She really *is* beautiful. *101 Dalmatians* was one of my favourite movies when I was little. Gracie preferred *Charlotte's Web*, but that was too sad for me.

'My neighbour. We're getting paid to look after her all day,' says Belle. 'Like doggy daycare.'

'Could … could that be an idea?' asks Maisie. 'Could we make, like, an actual doggy daycare business? A professional one? I could make us a website for people to book in and whatever.'

We look at each other, grinning like idiots. This isn't just Thinking Fire. This is like a Thinking Volcano. And you know what? It could actually work.

In half an hour, we've got the whole thing sorted – even the name, which is (drumroll please) Paws For Thought. (Get it?!) If it's a success, we'll have enough money at the end of each day to get the supplies we'll need for the next day's work. It doesn't take us long to decide who takes which role. Belle's the Company President, which means she's in charge of 'overseeing operations', which I secretly think just means bossing people.

Lola is Head of Marketing, which means she'll design our logo and flyers. She's already made us an Instagram account and posted four times to tell people that Paws For Thought is open for business and we're raising money to save Corner Park Clubhouse. It's so nice seeing her sketch out the possible logos in Belle's notebook. It sounds cheesy, but I reckon Lola was born to do art.

Maisie is Head of Technology. In about three seconds, she's made us a website on her iPad where clients can contact us.

'A stupid person couldn't do that,' I whisper, and she smiles. 'Hey – you're still here! You didn't go to gym!'

Maisie winks at me. 'Yup.'

'We're using your phone number,' Belle says to Lola. 'Obviously.'

'Sure,' says Lola, smiling to herself. 'I think I'll finish this at home with my paints.'

I'm Chief Financial Officer, which means I'll deal with the money. I'm not sure that's a great idea, but I'll try.

We draw up some business rules. We'll start taking bookings today, and open for business tomorrow. Any PFT team members who show up late will be on Poop Duty. For an extra fee, we'll offer a styling service, which basically just means putting in ribbons and giving the pups mohawks.

'But hang on … if we're busy looking after lots of dogs, how will we have time to fix the clubhouse?' asks Maisie.

Oh. We hadn't thought of that. Hmm.

'I could always ask the Eco Worriers to help out,' says Belle.

'I know it's been said by every single person in Sunnystream,' says Lola, 'but you are an actual genius. That is the most brilliant –'

'LOLA,' screams someone across the park. 'ARE YOU WEARING MY MOON SHORTS?' That's got to be Tally.

We all look over at Lola. She's totally wearing the moon shorts, plus a black-and-white checked top and silver half-moon earrings. Uh-oh.

'I AM LITERALLY GOING TO KILL YOU.' Tally's sprinting over now. Tally's an even faster runner than Lola. She's two years older, I guess.

'Jeepers,' says Lola, scrambling to her feet, but she's too late.

'What have I told you about stealing my stuff?' Tally says, trying to literally pull the shorts off Lola, who's trying to dodge away. Tally has the coolest green velvet headwrap over her hair. I sort of want to try one on, but I bet it would look stupid. 'I need those for filming today.'

'What are you filming, Tally?' asks Belle, which is a distraction tactic – I can tell by her 'innocent listening' face. And it works.

Tally stops trying to dack her sister and comes over to explain. 'You know that song *Moon River*?' she asks. The others all nod but I'm clueless about music.

'Oh Soph, seriously? From that old movie *Breakfast at Tiffany's*?' she asks. 'It's a classic. You gotta come over for more movie nights. Well, I'm playing that on the uke and then my friend Brendan –'

'*Boy*friend,' says Lola cheekily.

'Whatever, brat. He's beatboxing underneath it while I sing and then at one point he's going to do freestyling over the top. We're doing it live, though, so it's sort of scary.'

That surprises me. Tally isn't the kind of person who seems like she'd ever be scared. She has so many subscribers on YouTube that I thought she'd be used to this kind of thing. 'Exactly how many subscribers do you have now?' I ask.

'The numbers don't matter,' Tally says to me.

'Ha!' says Lola. 'Liar! You check them, like, every twenty minutes.'

Tally growls and goes back to trying to get the shorts. Then she and Lola start sort of clawing at each other's faces and wrestling. Eventually Lola breaks free.

'You can't – take – the shorts,' she pants. 'I'm wearing – saggy – undies.'

'Should have thought of that before,' says Tally, making a snatch.

They sprint off into the clubhouse.

'We don't have time for this,' Belle grumbles as we follow. 'We're businesswomen on the verge of a funding breakthrough.'

'Whoa,' Tally says, stopping in the middle of the hall and looking round at all the broken bits of floorboards and the cobwebs and grime and broken plaster, and the stage curtains that are ragged like torn ship sails. 'When did this place become such a dump?'

And then, as she hears what her voice sounds like, 'WHOA! Listen to these acoustics! I'd forgotten how great they are.' She pauses. 'You know, this was the first place I ever sang solo on stage?' She sings the first few lines of *Moon River* really loudly and they ring all around us, strong and pure and clear. Like we're standing inside a speaker. I do recognise it after all. We all stop to listen – even the dogs. It's beautiful.

'What are you guys doing here, anyway?' Tally asks when we've finished clapping, and she sounds like she's genuinely curious.

We look at each other cautiously, not sure how Lola will react. She can get weird about Tally. I think it's a jealousy thing.

'You can tell her,' says Lola. 'She's actually pretty great with advice.'

We all sit down on the edge of the stage and take turns with the story. By the time Tally's finished hearing about the Muscle Tower and Pony Soprano and the bulldozer, she is pretty wild with anger. 'You only have *how* long? *Five* days? And you need *how* much money?' We tell her and she whistles in disbelief.

'No offence,' she says slowly, like a plan is forming in her mind that second, 'but I think you're doing this all wrong. You need to get people involved *now* – before you've finished the whole clean-up. This needs to go viral. You need an action campaign. You need a petition to present to that buttwipe mayor to show that people aren't gonna put up with this sh– ... kind of thing. This clubhouse, it's like a little palace of memories. It's like ...' She trails off and looks around. 'Can I record in here? Today, I mean? Is there anywhere I could hang upside down? I know it won't have my towel rail, but is there something else?'

We all start hunting. It's Maisie who spots an old trapeze hanging from the ceiling above the stage.

'It's perfect,' Tally says.

'How would you get up there?' I ask.

'Is it safe?' Lola asks as she scratches Sergeant's belly. 'We need someone who knows about trapezes or, like, circus things.'

The same thought hits us all at the exact same moment: PUNK SHERMAN.

'No,' says Belle. 'I can't bear it. I can't involve him in my life. I can't owe him anything.'

'Think about Pony Soprano,' says Maisie.

'Think about the clubhouse,' says Lola.

'Think about what we're trying to do,' I say. 'He might be the only person in the whole town who knows this sort of stuff. Please?'

The rest, as they say, is history. We frantically scrub till our fingers are raw. Bit by bit, the place starts to sparkle, and two hours later, when the sun streams in through the little coloured windows, it makes patterns on the freshly mopped floor, like a kaleidoscope.

'I could fix up all these old lights,' says Punk when he's tightened all the bolts and confirmed the trapeze could hold a gorilla, and brought a giant ladder with him to attack the cobwebs on the ceiling. 'Get them all working again.'

'No thanks,' says Belle briskly. 'Your work here is done. Goodbye.'

Punk looks kind of hurt. 'Well, OK then, me bonny ladies,' he says sadly. 'I'll be off.' Punk Sherman calls us all kind of weird stuff like 'me bonny ladies' and 'the old queen bees'. Belle says he's using outdated gendered language. I think he might be trying to be friendly. I secretly like him because his front teeth stick so far out that he looks like a goofy beaver. I think she should give him a chance. Maybe he could make her mum really happy.

'Belle, I think … It would be good to have the lights working, wouldn't it?' I ask. 'In terms of, ah, making this a world-class performance space?'

'Huh,' says Belle. She loves things to be world-class. She can't argue with that.

Punk knows how to make the lights project stars onto the back of the stage. Brendan arrives with his DJ decks and Tally's ukulele. Tally hangs upside down in the moon shorts (after swapping clothes with Lola) and strums the ukulele like it's the easiest thing in the world. When they do the practice run, Clover wanders into the shot and starts to howl along. You'd think that would be a disaster, but it's weirdly beautiful and sort of haunting. So Brendan picks her up and sits her on a chair next to his decks so she can be on camera. She looks great on camera.

'Can you do the filming, Loles?' asks Tally. 'Oh, and this might sound better with some back-up instruments. Maybe call Rishi and see if he's free. Actually, can you get him to call Jules? I think the banjo would go well with this, too.'

'Can you mention our dogwalking business?' asks Belle. 'It's called Paws For Thought. People can start contacting us tomorrow via our website.'

'I don't usually do ads,' says Tally. 'It cheapens my

personal brand. But I guess I could make an exception.'

Fifteen minutes later, the band boys are here. Apparently the album isn't going that well and they're looking for any excuse to get away from it.

'I should go to gym,' Maisie whispers to me as RexRoy are tuning up their instruments and I'm looking over at Rishi, who's adjusting the height of the cymbal on his drum kit. She's bouncing on her toes, up and down, up and down.

'Stay,' I whisper back and circle my fingers around her little wrist. 'This is guaranteed never going to happen again. It's going to be incredible.'

'Can't,' she says, but I know from how she wrinkles her nose that she's only pretending she doesn't care. And also from the fact that when she's halfway to the bus stop, she turns around and comes back and arrives at the exact perfect moment, just as Tally starts to sing.

Truly, this is one of the prettiest songs I have ever heard. My arms get goosebumps. When it comes to Brendan's part, he does a rap about standing up for what you believe in with the banjo in the background. As the last note rings out, we smile at each other, Lola and Maisie and Belle and me.

Tally is still hanging upside down as she explains that the mayor is going to bulldoze our town's oldest building. 'If you care about justice,' Tally says, speaking straight into the camera. 'If you care about the little guy. If you care about giant A-holes taking over our communities, you need to be involved. Sign our online petition. Maybe you can even donate to our crowdfunding campaign at tallyupsidedown. com. And starting from tomorrow, google Paws For Thought at Corner Park for expert canine care in the Sunnystream area. I'm Tally. It's been real.' That's always her sign-off.

'What's "crowdfunding"?' Maisie asks.

'When anyone can give money to something by donating online,' I explain.

Within an hour, we have 2000 signatures. Two thousand! There's no guarantee that those people live in Sunnystream or even know where it is. It doesn't mean they'll actually show up at the rally – it's easy to just click a button, my dad always says, and harder to get your butt off your chair. But we're hopeful. Maybe, just maybe, this is going to all work out fine.

We're pulling weeds out of the garden when an old dark-green ute pulls up to the clubhouse.

'Is that Mikie?' I ask, squinting. It sure looks like his truck.

'Hey, team!' he calls as he jumps out of the ute and

slips on a patch of mud, landing on his butt. He tries to stand up and he slips again, this time onto his belly. Rishi and Tally laugh so much, they're actually crying, but not in a mean way, and Mikie smiles an aren't-I-an-idiot smile.

'I borrowed a cement mixer!' he calls when he's actually standing up again.

'Mikie's a carpenter,' I whisper to Belle. 'Does he know how to do cement? I don't think it's the same.'

'I sent him some YouTube tutorials,' says Belle. 'I'll supervise.'

As well as the cement mixer, Mikie's brought the coffee cart on the back of his ute, and he makes us all a hot chocolate before he starts work on the steps. We all sit around chatting – Rishi and Jules, Tally and Brendan, Clover, Punk and Mikie, Lola and Belle and Maisie and Sergeant and me. Rishi leans over and swaps my white marshmallows for his pink ones. How does he even –? He winks at me and I might actually be dead. I am probably writing this from heaven and I don't even realise.

But then we hear a beeping sound, like a giant alarm clock is going off in Corner Park. And then something massive comes into view …

A bulldozer – a giant one. Big and menacing, like a meat-eating dinosaur. It pulls up next to the clubhouse fence and shudders to a stop. My heart kind of shudders too.

CHAPTER 9

'There are eight dogs booked in on the website!' Maisie says the next morning as we stand in the dapply autumn sun. 'With Clover and Sergeant, that's ten! Not bad for the first day.'

We celebrate by eating the white-chocolate-and-banana muffins that I made last night. I figured we'd need snacks to get us through Step 3: Operation Undercoat. Lola has made something too: little bulldozer earrings. I smile as I spot them. They're only small, but somehow they make me feel stronger. Maisie has brought water bowls for the dogs and some rope for them to play tug-of-war. I've baked some doggy bone biscuits from a recipe online and brought my music box to hold the money, plus Togsley.

Four of the Eco Worriers have come to help out, and Belle is in full leadership mode as she prepares them for the task ahead.

'It was Julius Caesar who said *Veni, Vidi, Vici*, which is Latin for *I came, I saw, I conquered*,' she tells them. 'And from his shining example, we –'

'What's Latin?' asks a kid called Hattie.

Lola turns to me and Maisie and rolls her eyes as Belle launches into an explanation of dead languages. Sergeant begs me for a bit of my muffin. 'Nope, not for you, buddy,' I tell him. 'And you neither,' I tell Togsley, who is looking up at me with pleading eyes. 'Chocolate is poisonous for dogs. Go play with Clover.' Clover is trying to catch a fly in her mouth. Belle was right. She is actually really stupid.

Mikie arrives with his cart so he can serve coffee to our Paws For Thought customers. He parks it on the edge of the oval and comes over to check out the steps he finished yesterday. 'Sweet. I didn't even face-plant into the wet concrete or anything.' He grins and steps backwards, admiring his handiwork. Unfortunately he steps on Clover's paw and she yelps so loudly that Mikie jumps to the side and falls into a lavender bush.

'You're going to have to keep the dogs on leads at all times,' Belle tells the Eco Worriers, frowning over at Mikie. 'Or they're going to get in the way of our important work. And keep them away from that bulldozer, too. Ten dogs means how many each?' she quizzes.

The Eco Worriers just look at her with big eyes. Belle sighs.

But then we're all distracted by what's coming across the oval. Dogs. But not eight of them. There are ... heaps. Like, I can't even count them. This is like a scene from *101 Dalmatians*. And they're all headed for the clubhouse.

'What the ...' breathes Lola.

Maisie grabs her iPad from her backpack. 'The website said eight!' she says frantically, tapping on things in a panic. 'Unless – oh. It's crashed. *Error due to excess traffic.*'

'Traffic like cars?' asks the Eco Worrier called Paige.

'No, it means too many people tried to get onto the website and it had a meltdown,' Lola explains. 'Oh brother – here they come.'

The dogs and their owners, who must have all seen Tally's YouTube video, pour into the garden as Belle clambers to the top of the steps and waves her arms. 'Form an orderly queue,' she yells, and to us she says, 'Maisie, take down their details. Lola, fill up the water bowls. Soph, you handle the cash. Eco Worriers, stand next to Maisie and take the dogs once they're checked in.'

Belle really is a living, breathing Hermione Granger. Her plan works perfectly. The owners – including some who have come all the way from Cloud Town – start lining up neatly. The first twenty or so dogs get booked in, the Eco Worriers hold onto them like pros, and soon my music box won't shut with all the five-dollar notes that are shoved in there. Lola hands out muffins and charms everyone into upgrading to the dog-styling service. The Lola Effect is in full force.

'How are we going to have time to do all these mohawks?' I whisper to her between customers.

'Just think about the cash,' she whispers back.

'Hello, Tally,' says an elderly woman in a bright pink padded jacket with a dog called Spider, who is the size of Pony Soprano. An Irish wolfhound, I think they're called. 'I heard about this business on your YouTube channel. I love the post where you sang about crumpets, too.'

Uh-oh. Lola and Tally *do* look kind of similar, and Lola HATES it when people mix them up. (The crumpet post was also one of my personal favourites.)

'I'm not Tally. I'm Lola,' says Lola politely.

'Does Spider have any allergies?' asks Maisie quickly, filling in his information sheet on the iPad.

'Are you sure?' the lady asks Lola, which, truth be told, is sort of a dumb question.

'I'm sure,' says Lola through gritted teeth, not quite so politely.

'Well, are you and Tally twins?' the lady asks. 'I didn't know she had a twin. I know about the famous brother, but there's no twin on her Wikipedia page. Spider is allergic to bad cosmic energy,' she tells Maisie as she hands his lead to Hattie, the Eco Worrier who is also holding onto the leads of a cavoodle, a bulldog and two chihuahuas.

'How do I spell "cosmic"?' Maisie whispers to me.

'How it sounds,' I whisper back.

'That doesn't help,' says Maisie.

Lola glares at the lady. 'Have a muffin,' she says tightly, thrusting one into the lady's face in a way that I'd describe as bordering on aggressive.

But because Spider is so tall, he just rips it right out of Lola's hand. Hattie is so surprised, she drops his lead, as well as all the other leads she's holding. The dogs chase Spider and his muffin over to the sundial, where he bares his teeth. I don't blame him. I don't want to brag, but those muffins are sort of epic. A chow chow called Mavis bares her teeth back at Spider, and heaps of the dogs start yelping. The pups that the other Eco Worriers are holding start jumping and barking and straining at their leads. The dogs that are still in the queue – another twenty of them, maybe – start howling and yipping. Their owners start to call out things like, 'Hey, calm down! It's fine,' but the whole place suddenly feels jangly. I wouldn't have been able to describe it before, but now I realise that it's full of bad cosmic energy.

Spider chomps down the last of the muffin and then turns and bounds over towards Mikie's coffee cart. I bet he's sniffed out the marshmallows. Clover joins him, and together they jump up, putting their paws on the edge where the milk jug is waiting.

'Tally, don't let Spider near the milk!' his owner shrieks at Lola as she sprints after them. 'He only drinks soy!'

But Lola is too late. Clover and Spider are BIG dogs, and the weight of their paws tips the coffee cart over backwards with a huge crash. The wheel axle breaks. The generator goes flying onto the grass. The sack of coffee beans splits open. Mavis and the chihuahuas and three different Labradors race over and start eating them, their leads flying behind them. The Eco

Worriers panic and drop the leads they were holding, and canines go running everywhere.

Within three seconds, a husky called Montana is digging up the vegetable patch. I'm ashamed to say that Togsley joins him, and so do about ten other dogs, until dirt is flying around like sand in a desert storm. A Doberman called Prince William is trying to chew the side of the clubhouse – chew through the actual wood! Two beagles are playing tug-of-war with Olivia's hoodie and she's crying.

'That's my favourite hoodie,' she weeps. 'Please – do something!'

But when I try to pull it out of the dogs' mouths, it rips in half. Eek.

People are tripping up. Leads are getting tangled around drainpipes and bannisters and fence posts. There's snarling and whimpering and a LOT of barking. Mikie tries to tackle Spider, who is running off with an entire tin of seventy-per-cent-cocoa Dutch hot chocolate powder, which Judy imported specially from Belgium. Mikie misses and dives headfirst into one of the water bowls.

It's *full* doggy chaos.

I look around to find Belle, who surely must have a plan, even for this kind of mayhem, and spot her climbing up onto the bulldozer, right onto its roof. She stands up and puts her fingers into her mouth and whistles – the longest, loudest wolf whistle I have ever heard. Everyone flings their hands up to their ears. The dogs stop dead still in their tracks.

'ATTENTION!' yells Belle. 'ATTENTION! RETURN TO YOUR HOUSES! PAWS FOR THOUGHT IS OFFICIALLY CLOSED.'

CHAPTER 10

'I don't get this,' says Maisie later that afternoon. She and Belle are sitting on the stage doing two-variable equations while Lola and I paint the walls with the last of the undercoat. That's a type of maths. The equations, not the undercoat. The undercoat is the type of paint you put on to get the walls ready for the proper paint colour, the top layer, which we're still yet to choose. Mikie was supposed to be taking us to the Hard Hair Store tonight to decide. Judy was going to come around and help, too, and bring us pizza from Rita's. But none of that's happening now.

Maisie is gloomy about the maths and we're all gloomy about the bulldozer that's sitting outside, reminding us time's a-ticking, and don't even get me started on the whole money situation. It took the whole morning to clean up the mangled garden after the Paws For Thought fiasco and we had to give the money back, though people were really nice about it. Then we had to pay Mikie for the damage to the coffee cart – who knew wheel axles were so pricey? – and buy Olivia a new hoodie. And we could only do *that* because Lola sold her entire collection of earrings to Pepper Peters from the Cloud Town Cougars. She's the captain, and even though you're supposed to have short nails when you play netball, boy does she *scratch*. Watching Lola hand over the earrings in a shoebox was even more painful than watching Pepper hold her nose when she walked into the clubhouse. I guess it does smell kind of damp and mouldy but you get used to it pretty quickly.

With the money left over, we could only afford enough undercoat to do the bottom half of the walls, so now the bottom half looks sort of OK and the top half is still the colour of old teeth. It's not the professional look we were going for.

'What about the crowdfunding?' Maisie asks Lola. 'Aren't we making money from that?'

'The thing about crowdfunding is that people pay *after* you reach the goal,' says Lola, who today has on this incredible dress she sewed from a flowery brown couch cushion cover that her grandma was going to throw away. She literally just made a hole in each end and tied it with a pearly-pink belt but it looks like something you'd see on a vlog. It's weird seeing her with no earrings on. 'You can do the maths on this, Killer. We need –'

'Stop distracting her,' Belle says grumpily. 'If she doesn't get to the Olympics, it's going to be your fault.'

Maisie groans. 'I am literally *never* going to get this. We may as well give up now.'

'You will too get it,' Belle tells her. 'Remember, Mais: *if you're going through hell, keep going.*'

'Shakespeare?' I ask as I run the roller up and down the walls.

'Fake Winston Churchill again,' says Belle. 'So who knows?'

'I'm so dumb I don't even remember who that is,' groans Maisie.

'You're not!' we all say together.

'Can you say it again?' asks Lola.

'I'm so dumb –' Maisie begins.

'Not that, Mais – the Churchy thing,' says Lola.

'Can you not Instagram that and just keep painting?' snaps Belle.

'No no,' says Lola earnestly. 'I'm not going to post it. I just want to know. For me.'

Since we started fixing up the clubhouse, Lola's been making a time-lapse video. That means her phone's been sitting in a corner filming everything, so she hasn't been able to use it. Now she's out of the habit, she doesn't seem to care as much anymore.

'It's like, when I try to read the questions, the letters move around,' says Maisie. 'Is that weird?'

'WHAT?' says Belle. 'You've never told me that. Maisie, that sounds like you have dyslexia.'

'Dis-what-ia?' asks Maisie.

'I mean, I'm no expert. But I've read pretty much everything about it online. So I sort of am. The science behind it is actually quite fascinating. Neural pathways –'

There's a knock at the still-broken door and a low voice. 'Yello?'

'Thank goodness,' Lola mutters, and secretly I feel the same. Sometimes it's hard to keep up with Belle's brain.

'Coach Jack!' says Maisie – in a shocked way, not an excited way. Which is weird. Coach Jack's her favourite coach. There's something else in her voice, but I can't quite put my finger on it.

Coach Jack almost has to duck his head when he walks through the clubhouse door.

'Aren't you too tall to be a gymnast?' Lola asks in her talking-to-a-boy voice.

'Lucky I grew late. After the Olympics. Hey gang,' says Coach Jack, and he glances around at the patchy walls, looking sort of confused. 'Are you doing your own home make-over show in here?'

'It doesn't look that good because we can't afford the paint yet,' says Lola, and she does this thing where she dips her head and looks up through her eyelashes. She does have pretty great eyelashes, like a baby deer. 'This is just the undercoat.'

'Well, that explains where you've been, Killer. I had a hunch it might be here. You thought I wouldn't notice you were gone, hey?'

'What do you mean?' Belle frowns.

'This one's skipped two days of Holiday Hell,' he says to us, pointing at Maisie. 'That's our holiday intensive course for the elite squad. Actually, she's skipped three days including today. Does your mum know about this?' he asks Maisie. 'We've got State Champs coming up in a few months …'

What?! We all turn to look at Mais, and BOY does she look guilty. I feel guilty, too, for getting her to stay these past couple of days. But I didn't know about Holiday Hell. It sounds important. Also quite hard.

'I just wanted to help,' she says, all defensive. 'And sometimes … I dunno.' I love that I know Maisie so well I know what her 'dunno' means here. It means that sometimes she feels like she gives up so much stuff for gymnastics and she just wants to be a normal kid. But that SHE'S the one who's always fighting to be allowed to be a gymnast, so she feels like she has to do her total best, all the time, to prove to her parents that it's worth it – the time, the money, everything. Poor Maisie. It's all kind of complicated.

'Zhang Ai Mei!' Belle says crossly. (That's Maisie's Chinese name.) 'Why didn't you say anything? We could have managed without you.'

'But I love this place,' she says, looking round. 'It reminds me of being a kid and … I dunno. Being free.'

'Well, enjoy it while you can,' Belle sighs. 'Because this time next week, it's going to be a pile of planks.'

'What do you mean?' asks Coach Jack.

'Didn't you see Tally's song on YouTube?' Belle asks. 'Lola, we clearly need to expand our marketing efforts. Our campaign message is obviously not being heard.'

Lola glares. 'Um, I've been kind of busy? I did the flyers about the rally last night, didn't I? Coach Jack, have you seen any flyers around town?'

'Oh – actually, someone put something on my windscreen today, under the wipers. And all the other cars in town. Was that you guys?'

'No,' says Lola, 'ours were just on the noticeboard at Buck's and around the gazebo at Handkerchief Place.'

'And the Eco Worriers wouldn't have put them on people's cars without asking,' says Belle. She has them SUPER well-trained.

'I think I chucked it on my front seat,' says Coach Jack. 'Let me grab it.'

He comes back with a really glossy flyer, printed on both sides. It's definitely not one of ours. '*Once in a lifetime opportunity,*' he reads from the huge letters at the top. '*SHARK TANK – MONDAY – 10AM. BIG PRIZE! Be there!*'

'WHAT!' we yell.

'What opportunity?' demands Belle, ripping it out of Coach Jack's hand. She reads the rest out to us. '*One dish served on Monday between 10am and 11am will have a golden ticket underneath it entitling the lucky customer to a LIFETIME's supply of pancakes at Ja-pancake Par-LA!. Be in it to win it. See you there!*' She crumples it up and throws it on the ground – throws it *hard*. Then she lets out a T-Rex-sized roar.

Coach Jack flinches, looking confused.

Lola starts taking these really deep breaths, like she's Darth Vader from *Star Wars*.

I get it. I can't stress to you enough how much people LOVE those pancakes. Heck, *I* love those pancakes. Come Monday, that's where everyone's going to be. Mayor Magnus wouldn't be smart enough to plan this, but do you know who would?

'Bart Strabonsky,' whispers Maisie, shaking her head.

'The dude with the eyeglass thingy? Killer, what are you talking about?' says Coach Jack. 'What is going on here?'

'Monday at ten is right when our rally is,' I say in almost a whisper. 'That's when the clubhouse is going to be torn down.'

'What?! What do you mean, "torn down"?' says Coach Jack. 'Wait – THAT'S what the bulldozer's for?! But that's crazy! There's no Sunnystream without the clubhouse. I mean, I haven't been here in ages, but still ...'

As he says it, I realise there's this weird disconnect between people loving the idea of the clubhouse and actually going there. It reminds me of something my dad always says. Said. 'There is no love – there are only proofs of love.' I think it means that unless you show you care, you're not actually being caring. And the whole of Sunnystream has forgotten to care for the clubhouse. Even WE forgot to care for it before this whole thing happened.

'And you know what?' Coach Jack continues. 'This is where my grandpa came every day when he got back from the war. It's where they came to remember the dudes who didn't make it. I think they taught classes here for the returned soldiers.'

'That's right. Woodcrafts and beekeeping,' says Belle knowledgeably. 'I read about it in *Sunnystream: A History*. Would you like to borrow the book? It's an inspiring example of thoroughly researched local history.'

'Er, sure,' says Coach Jack. 'Look, I really shouldn't be doing this,' he tells Maisie, 'but take the rest of the week off – regular training too. Just don't tell your mum. She's paid for it but I'll figure that out next term. Stupid Magnus. And make sure you keep up a bit of balance work in the meantime, OK? Nothing too tricky, though – no flip combos without a mat.'

'Will you be here on Monday at ten?' says Lola. 'For our rally?'

'Monday's kind of a tricky day, isn't it?' asks Coach

Jack. 'I mean, I'll try my best, but I'll have to get out of my shift at the gym. It's gonna be hard for people with jobs and businesses and all that.'

Oh. We hadn't thought about that. You can almost hear the last sparks of our Big Idea fizzle out.

'But you never know,' Coach Jack continues, trying to sound enthusiastic, like he's realised he's crushed our dreams. 'I'll put it on Facebook. And hey, if you need a hand around the place, I'm great with a drill.' He looks at the top half of the walls and frowns. And then tries to not frown. 'See you, girls. Catch you, Killer.'

Maisie smiles, but it's a stressed kind of smile. 'Not if I catch you first.'

As Coach Jack is leaving, he stops and turns and looks at me – straight at me. 'Soph,' he says. 'I'm really sorry about Gracie. You hang in there, OK?'

I can feel my face blazing. I swallow. 'Thanks, Coach Jack.' I want to say something else – I feel like I *need* to say it. The words are all there in my head, lined up: *Gracie, she really liked you. She thought you were the best coach in any sport she ever had. She thought you were like a big, smart, handsome bear. Thank you for being in her life. It wasn't a very long life, but you helped make it special.*

But the words just won't come out.

He nods and stands for a minute, gazing out the newly cleaned windows like he's looking at something that isn't there. 'She was a good one,' he says quietly. Then he leaves, and I have the wishing feeling again.

I can feel the others watching me and looking at each other, wincing like I'm causing them actual pain.

I walk outside, through the back door to the garden, and sit down against the Japanese maple. Its red leaves wave like little hands. Like tiny fluttering hearts. I can't bear to think of it being flattened by that bulldozer, cracked through as if it had been split by lightning. I rest my head against the trunk and close my eyes. My throat hurts with all the words that are still jammed inside.

Someone comes over and rests their head next to mine. We stay like that for a while, me and whoever it is. 'Want to sleep over tonight?' Belle asks eventually. 'Actually, do you all want to sleep over?' she calls to the others.

To get how incredibly kind that is, you have to know that Belle doesn't like having people over to her house. She's never said it directly, but I think she's embarrassed about where she lives.

'Yes!' says Maisie, and Lola sort of whoops. 'Who's got The Jar?'

'I do,' I say, though I haven't thought about it in months. 'I'll get it when I fetch my sleeping bag from home.'

Belle checks her watch and squeezes my knee. 'Come on. Let's swing by town and see what's happened to our flyers while we get supplies.' She reaches over and wipes away the tears that are mid-way through their slip down my face. 'I carry your heart,' she whispers.

And I whisper back, 'I carry it in my heart.'

CHAPTER 11

The main street is plastered with the pancake flyers – they're covering literally every surface. Not a single one of Lola's is anywhere. And here's the worst part. Well, one of the many bad parts. We didn't read the other side of the one Coach Jack had, but on the reverse is a picture of the clubhouse with a giant red cross through it. *DANGER*, it says. *CONDEMNED! STAY AWAY!*

'What's "condemned"?' asks Maisie.

'That means it's not safe to go near,' says Belle.

'But Mr Morrison said it was fine!' says Lola. 'They're just trying to stop people coming to the protest. The

126

competition's one thing, but this is just lies!'

Grey Dare walks past, holding a flyer. He waves it at us and says, 'Hey. You girls going to enter the pancake comp? I freaking love that wasabi mayonnaise, hey.'

'Um, NO!' says Belle, kind of hysterically. 'Haven't you heard about the clubhouse?'

'How it's haunted?' he asks. 'Crazy, isn't it! Who'd have thunk?'

'What do you mean, *haunted*?' asks Maisie. 'Who told you that?'

Grey Dare looks confused, maybe about how intense we're all acting. 'Um, the band boys, maybe? Apparently Pony Soprano won't go near there because he can see ghosts.'

'WHAT?' we all yell together.

'Oh yeah – that's why Mayor Magnus is moving the clubhouse to a nice farm out of town. Thank goodness. I thought that guy was a bit of an idiot, but he sure must love Pony Soprano.'

We just stare at each other, gobsmacked, as Grey Dare slinks away looking kind of terrified.

My old ballet teacher, Miss Claudine, walks past, trying to juggle her fruit and vegetables without a bag. She sees us all holding the flyers. 'Oh!' she says in her lovely gentle voice. I miss that voice. 'I heard that part of the clubhouse roof fell on Mikie's coffee cart and broke it in half. Poor thing.'

'That's NOT what happened!' yells Lola, and Miss Claudine jumps backwards in shock, dropping a bunch of kale and some mandarins. As if on cue, the Eco Worriers appear and pick them all up for her.

'Good job you're here,' Belle barks at them. 'We're taking down every single one of these pancake flyers. And then we're burning them in a massive bonfire. Starting NOW.'

'Shouldn't we recycle them?' asks Olivia, and they all look kind of worried.

'Isn't burning printed paper going to release toxic fumes?' asks Hattie.

'Just go fetch them,' growls Belle.

'Isobelle, those kids are not dogs,' says Lola. 'Have some respect.'

'We need to start a major education campaign,' fumes Belle. 'We need to visit every shop and business and give them the facts. We can't let them fall for this treasonous propaganda.'

'Trees and us ... what?' asks Maisie.

'Miss Claudine,' I say to Miss Claudine. 'Let me tell you the truth about what's happening to Corner Park Clubhouse.'

'OMG, Francine, I LOVE that!' says Lola as we all traipse in to Belle's house late in the afternoon. 'Can I take a photo?'

There is literally nothing in the tiny, tiny living room except a chair, paints and canvases, buckets and brushes, and the picture that Belle's mum, Francine, is painting. It's of fluoro-pink horses galloping through a supermarket. I can see why Lola loves it. It's bright and wild, sort of like her. All of Francine's pictures have colourful horses in interesting places, like space and a bowling alley.

'Sure, doll face,' says Francine. 'Snap away. Are you guys here for some of Punk's famous pulled pork?'

Doll face. Where have I heard that before?

'For the zillionth time, I'm a gosh-darn vegetarian,' says Belle. 'And we've brought our own supplies, seeing as I knew there'd be nothing here.' Her eyebrows are so close together that they're almost joined. When she's really mad, they almost cross.

Belle and her mum are sort of … really different. They fight all the time. It reminds me of lightsabers clashing into each other, like in *Star Wars*. Belle's mum doesn't buy groceries very often – or anything, really, like furniture or clothes. She doesn't tidy up. Gracie once said that's why Belle's a total control freak – because her mum is chaotic. I think it's got something to do with Belle's dad, who we've never met and who she never, *ever* talks about.

They also have what Belle describes as 'a unique living situation'. Their house is tall and narrow and sort of, well, falling apart. There's a bedroom in the basement, and a living room on the ground level (that's where we are now) and then an attic that's Belle's bedroom up some rickety stairs. There's a hole in her ceiling, so you can see the stars, but it does get kind of cold in winter, and drippy, so it's always full of saucepans and bowls to catch the rain. Her room is so tiny that when Belle's in bed and the rest of us lie on the floor, we take up the entire room, squished together. It's what my mum would call 'a renovator's delight'.

'Is that me bonny ladies?' Punk calls from the kitchen, which is really just a hot plate in a cupboard. It's amazing what Belle can cook on there, though. (Francine never cooks anything.) Punk pops his head out. He's wearing all black leather, except for an apron that says 'Quiche the Chef'. 'Yo!' he says through the beaver teeth.

'Yo, Punk!' says Maisie.

'That smells good,' says Lola.

'Did you know that pigs are smarter than dogs?' says Belle darkly.

'Well, stone the crows,' he says happily. 'Sure I can't tempt you?'

'No thanks,' we say, sort of reluctantly, because it smells amazing. But do you know what else is amazing? What's in our overnight bags.

Seven minutes later, we've lugged all our stuff upstairs, including The Jar, which I dropped by home to get, along with my sleeping bag and sleepover stuff. Mum wasn't there, but when is she ever really there? I left her a note. Now we're all in our PJs, surrounded by all the food that you're not supposed to eat for dinner, which we picked up from Buck's with the fifty dollars Mum gave me for dinner a few days ago that I'd forgotten about.

'Shouldn't we be using this for paint?' Maisie asked when we were at the check-out. But even Belle agreed that if ever we needed a cheeky cheer-up, it was tonight.

This is what you can get for not even fifty dollars: cheese corn chips, and Maltesers, and jelly snakes, and those Furry Friend chocolates in the little rectangles with the cute pictures on the front, and sour worms, and milk bottles, and a box of mini Magnum ice-creams, and Pringles (the green ones), and a bag of Milky Ways, and some white bread and butter and hundreds-and-thousands that I am currently making into fairy bread, and a box of Barbecue in a Biskit. We actually can't finish it all. By the end, I feel so full that I have to lie down.

We've agreed not to talk about all the things we still have to do to save the clubhouse – not tonight. It's too depressing. So the first person to mention the clubhouse has to do a dare that may or may not involve undies on their head. Belle schedules a fundraising brainstorm to be held over breakfast tomorrow when we're fresh.

After today, there are only three days left and the walls are still half brown and half white because we can't afford the undercoat – or the paint. The windows are still cracked and one has no glass in it, the door's still broken, the curtains still look like they've been attacked by slash-happy pirates. We talked to heaps of people about the rally, so I guess that's something. Lots of them said they love the clubhouse but they're not sure they're going to be able to come on Monday because of work. A few just sighed and said, 'What's the point? That Mayor Magnus just does what he wants anyway.' And one of them asked if we could get Tally to sing at their daughter's bat-mitzvah party, which put Lola in a really snippy mood.

It's freezing at Belle's house with the wind coming in through the roof, and at one point we can't hear each other speak because Francine and Punk Sherman are singing REALLY loudly to songs by a band called Vampire Weekend, which of course I've never heard of. I think Belle's also pretty embarrassed that we can hear them call each other 'babe' all the time, because at one point she gets super crabby and accuses Maisie of cheating at Connect Four. But apart from that, it's just like old times.

We talk about our old teachers, and kids from our primary school that are at our new schools, though Belle has none at hers and Lola only has two. One of those is a girl called Ladybird who has an anxiety parrot, which is sort of like a guide dog for people who feel anxious. She has special permission to have it sit on her shoulder in class. The parrot's name is John West Junior.

Maisie confesses that at lunch she sits with two girls from the Cloud Town Cougars – our rival netball team, who always elbow us when the umpires aren't looking – so we all throw things at her, but only in a jokey way. I quickly change the subject so I don't have to confess that I sit with literally no-one. 'Hey,' I say. 'Is it time for Seven Questions?'

Even though we're too old for some things, like monkey bars and handstand competitions and four square and putting on plays, at least we haven't grown out of Seven Questions. It's a game we made up ourselves. It's sort of a cross between 'Truth or dare' and 'Would you rather' and 'Never have I ever'. We've been writing down lots of questions since we were in year four and putting them in this huge jar that used to hold five kilos of peanut butter, which is probably how much Lola's family could eat in one day. There must be hundreds of bits of different coloured paper scrunched up in there. You take turns picking from The Jar and reading out the question. Everyone writes down their answers on a piece of paper but they don't put their name on it. Once you've done seven questions, you all swap answers and read them out and try to guess who wrote what. If you like finding out stuff about your friends, I HIGHLY recommend it. You just have to practise disguising your handwriting, but we're good at that bit now. Belle gets us pens and paper, and we launch right in. Soon we're up to question five.

'Would you rather kiss Bart Strabonsky with full

tongue or wear underpants with grass seeds in them for a whole week?'

The way Lola is giggling, she totally wrote this one.

'GROSS,' says Belle. 'That is a completely inappropriate question.'

Her face is so disgusted that Maisie and I laugh until we have literal tears. I choose the grass seed underpants and I reckon Maisie does too. I bet Lola chooses kissing. She always chooses kissing. The rule is that you can't pass, so I bet Belle chooses the grass seeds.

Maisie picks out a green balled-up bit of paper. 'Truth: which person in this room do you like the most and why?'

Lola whistles.

'Whoa,' says Maisie. 'Great question.'

Belle frowns. 'Friendship's not a competition. But rules are rules. No passes.'

As I bend my head to answer, I try not to care that no-one will write my name down. They won't write Belle's either, but Belle couldn't care less. Lola seems kind of low-level annoyed at Belle these days, so she'll write Maisie. The others will write Lola because she's Lola. Something about Lola makes you want to be around her and be like her, and for her to like you. Even though Belle rolls her eyes about the Lola Effect,

I know she feels it as well. For a second, I think about writing Lola's name too.

But then I remember the thud on my bed when Maisie climbs through my window before training. How she once punched a boy called Massimo who cut off my ponytail on a dare in year four. How she took Lemon Tart to live at her house over the summer because she knew I couldn't look at her.

Maisie, I write. *Because she is ~~sweet thoughtful awesome~~ the actual best*.

It's my turn next, and I stick my hand in The Jar. The little ball of paper is yellow.

'What is the worst thing that's ever happened to you?' I read when I've unscrunched it.

Then there's that feeling like when your fridge stops humming, and you didn't realise how noisy it was until it goes quiet. Everyone is so still. But my friends don't look away like most people around town would.

I swallow.

I whisper, 'Can I pass?'

In the pause that follows, I can hear a dog barking, so far away it could be calling from another planet. I think about how Gracie was obsessed with that dog that the Russians sent into space. Her name was Little Curly.

'You could just try writing it, Soph,' Lola says, really gently. 'It might make you feel a little better.'

Maisie nods and squeezes my arm, and Belle says, 'She's right. When my new friend Matilda's grandma died …'

I get a scrunched-up feeling when she mentions Matilda, all jealous and tight.

Lola shoots her a death stare.

I look down at the lines on the page.

Slowly, my hand shaking, I write four words. Such little words, but together they're big.

The others cheer so loudly, I worry that Punk Sherman is going to want to come and join the fun. I blush. Lola is right. I *do* feel a little better. Maybe more than a little. Maybe a whole lot. As I smile down at the paper and the others lean in to hug me, something blooms in my chest – something warm and good. It takes me a moment to recognise it because I haven't had this feeling for so long. It's hope.

Suddenly I feel proud, like I want to tell someone I've been brave. That someone has springy grey curls and kind blue eyes. I realise I want to tell Dad.

'Let's not read these now. Let's go to the park,' Belle says, going over to her wardrobe. 'I've got marshmallows in here. We can light a fire and toast them.'

'WHAT?!' the rest of us say together.

'MORE sugar! Public fire-lighting in a banned area! Sneaking out at night unsupervised?!' says Lola. 'Who are you and where is Isobelle?!'

Belle shrugs as we wriggle out of our sleeping bags and start pulling on shoes and jumpers and beanies. 'Maisie doesn't have to get up for training. No more dogs to walk. We can stay out as late as we like.'

My mum would hate the idea, which sort of makes me want to do it more. That's bad, isn't it? But don't freak out too much, because Sunnystream is literally the safest place in the galaxy. There was an article about it recently in the local paper, the *Sunnystream Gazette*.

Outside, the moon is fully round, like a plate, and we take turns making our breath come out like dragon smoke. Maisie's glow-in-the-dark skeleton onesie looks amazing as she does handsprings across the oval. The rest of us run after her, giggling as the breeze whips our hair. When we swing past the playground, I go headfirst down the stegosaurus slide on my tummy, fast, my arms stretched wide. For the first time in forever, I feel light and I feel free.

At the clubhouse, we chicken out of making the fire. We're not really the biggest rule-breakers, I guess. So we sit on Mikie's smart new concrete steps and burn the marshmallows with matches. We go through a whole box, the flames nipping our fingers till we all have little blisters on the tips. It hurts but we don't care – it just feels so good being out here in the night-time. It feels like we're grown-up but also like we're heaps younger, both at the same time. The marshmallows are just the right amount of burnt and melty.

In the ghost-ring of torch glow, Belle puts aside all the pink ones for me. 'Gracie's favourite, right?' she asks. I smile at her in the starlight. 'Yep,' I say. 'Mine too.'

'Belle,' I say slowly after a while. 'Do you think I should talk to my dad? Did I make a mistake, not wanting to see him because he moved away?'

'Or did he make a mistake when he ran away from *you*?' she asks. 'He can try to come back into your life all he likes, but he still chose to leave.' She says it all with such force that I realise she's not even talking about my dad, Andy Hargraves, anymore. She's talking about another dad who left his daughter so far back that none of us ever knew him at all.

'What happened to your dad, Belle?' I say quietly, which I've never been brave enough to do before. Guess I'm on a roll tonight. Not even Lola knows about Belle's dad – I know because I've asked her. 'Do you know who he is? Has he tried to come back? Like, ever?'

Belle flicks the torch on and off, on and off. 'Oh, I know who he is,' she says after a while. 'And more than anything in this world, I wish I didn't.'

1. Ever told a lie to this group?
   Yes! Not saying what though.
2. What do you want to be when you grow up?
   Vet or baker.
3. Who is your crush?
   Tom Mullins (in my SOSE class).
4. Serve ice-cream at Judy's in the nude
   OR wet your pants at the Anzac Service?
   Wet pants, I guess?!?!
5. Grass seeds in your undies or kissing
   Bart Strabonsky (tongue)?
   Grass seeds!!
6. Person I like the most here:
   Maisie. Because she is ~~sweet~~ ~~thoughtful~~ ~~awesome~~
   the actual best.
7. The worst thing that ever happened:
   My twin sister died.

CHAPTER 12

'Sophia?' someone whispers to me through the dark. 'Soph?' That someone is Gracie. This is just how she whispers on Christmas morning when she wants to crack open our stockings.

'Hi,' I whisper back, smiling. It's so nice to hear her voice. 'What's the time?'

'Early o'clock,' she says. 'Go back to sleep. I'm just going out for a bit.'

'Don't go,' I whisper, feeling my eyes trying to open. But we must have stayed out late last night because they're stuck closed with the gunk I get when I'm super tired. 'OK, bye,' I whisper sleepily, already half stepping into a dream.

When I wake again, it's early but light. Lola and Belle are still snoozing, but Maisie's sleeping bag is empty. She's probably in the bathroom, which is downstairs next to the kitchen. I hope she got to sleep in at least a bit, because she pretty much never has the chance.

Gracie isn't there. Today will be another day without her, and I can't do anything about that. Nothing will ever bring her back. She'll never get older than twelve. But what I *can* do is live my life as a thank-you to Gracie for all the times we had together – I can be brave, and kind, and generous, like she was. As I stare out of the gap in the ceiling at the sunrise, I realise that saving Corner Park Clubhouse is the first step in doing that. Gracie loved that clubhouse. She really loved this town.

The pink clouds remind me of last night's marshmallows. We mustn't have eaten them that long ago, but already I feel hungry. Waffles pop into my head. I don't want to boast, but my waffles are pretty great. I wriggle out of my bag, trying to be as stealthy as Maisie. I could make waffles for everyone and we could sit around on the floor and eat them together, which is actually my idea of heaven, and think up ideas about how to pay for the paint. Surely Francine would have eggs and sugar and milk and flour? Hmm, on second thoughts, that's kind of a long list for someone who never shops.

I tiptoe down the stairs and through the living room to the tiny cupboard-kitchen. My fears are confirmed. I find pink Himalayan rock salt and a tiny case of saffron threads and a box of Confuse-ly, which looks like rabbit pellets but says it's a kind of muesli that Ancient Egyptians enjoyed. In the fridge there's a set of car keys (??) and a box of after-dinner mints.

Luckily for us, Buck's opens at six in the morning on Friday and I still have some change from last night. I wait for a bit to see if Maisie wants to come, but she's taking ages in the bathroom. So I slip out by myself, still in my cat-face pyjamas, hoping I don't bump into my mum. She's often out powerwalking about now, or at bootcamp. And she is so NOT OK with wearing PJs in public, or even outside. 'Like a pair of homeless people,' she'd say when Gracie and I wore our nighties on the trampoline. I flick the lock so it won't click when I pull the door closed. Maybe I'm the one who could be an assassin.

As I walk up to Handkerchief Place, there's nobody else around to see the dawn light turning from pink to apricot. The world seems gentle and it feels nice to be doing something for someone else. The waffles, I mean. But also fixing the clubhouse. I guess it's easier to do things to cheer up other people than it is to cheer yourself up. For me, anyway. Helping people helps yourself, my dad always says. As I walk around Buck's in my ugg boots, I wonder if he's at the gym in the city apartment or away in Los Angeles again. I wonder if he hates me or loves me. I wonder if he's ever coming home.

I get maple syrup and some half-price blueberries, too, and the guy on the cash register looks at me and looks sad and looks away. So I look away, too, at today's newspaper, which is in a big pile next to the counter. And I absolutely cannot *believe* what I am seeing. I snatch one up. 'This too,' I say quickly. I cannot WAIT to see Belle's face when she reads the headline.

When I'm three-quarters of the way back to her house, I realise someone is following me. I stop.

And whoever it is stops too. I start and they start. I stop and they stop. Holy smoke.

This isn't good.

I have that hammering heart thing that Belle always tells us is a part of our brains from way back when we were monkeys – I think it's called fight-or-flight mode. As I stand there, fear pumps through me and the waffles seem like a really dumb idea. Just when I'm thinking of ditching the groceries and making a sprint for it, someone says, 'Sophia?'

I turn around.

It's Patrick. Gracie's BFF.

Patrick and Gracie did literally everything together – except for the year Patrick was really into ballet, which totally wasn't Gracie's thing. She went and watched his concert, though. She said he was the best Tulip Waving in the Breeze that she'd ever seen. Patrick goes to my school, but to be honest, I've tried really hard to avoid him. Up until now I haven't felt brave enough to see him. But maybe now's the time to keep my brave streak from last night going.

'Remember when you were a tulip?' I ask as Patrick catches up to me. It's kind of a random thing to say after all this time, but he grins at me and I can't help smiling back. 'You scared me, by the way. You shouldn't follow people like that!'

'Sorry – didn't mean to,' says Patrick. 'I just never know if … if you want to talk to me.'

'It's not you.' I sigh. 'It's just that talking is hard. I always end up wanting to cry. Then I can't get the words out.'

'Nothing wrong with crying,' he says. 'Would be weird if you didn't, wouldn't it? Considering.'

I'd forgotten how easy it is to chat to Patrick. He used to spend so much time at our house that my dad built a third stool at the kitchen bench, just for him. My parents called him Pudge, which made no sense because he was as tall as Lola and really skinny, like he'd been stretched. He used to help us dress up Lemon Tart as famous people so we could film her – Sherlock Holmes, the Queen, Abraham Lincoln.

Patrick must be remembering that too, because he says, 'How's Lemon Tart?'

'She's still at Maisie's,' I say. 'But I miss her.' As I say it, I realise it's true. I miss that rabbit. I miss Gracie. And I miss this boy. 'I miss you, too. And having you over at ours. Who do you, like … hang out with now?'

Patrick looks uncomfortable, and I feel super guilty. I've been so wrapped up in my own head that I haven't thought about what it would be like to be him. How I'd feel if I lost Maisie, or Lola, or Belle. Like the stars had gone out, I bet. It would be hard to find someone else to be that close with again.

'You should come over sometime, Pudge,' I say as we reach Belle's gate. 'I'll make you waffles. Bring Cheeks.'

'I'd like that. And hey, come find me at lunch when school's back. I'm in the library, usually.'

I smile. 'Reading Party?'

Patrick smiles back. 'Deal. Hey – I saw the flyers about the clubhouse. That's cool, what you're doing. Let me know if I can help.'

'Deal. You don't know how to raise a whole heap of money, do you? Like, really fast?'

Patrick looks at me for a moment, his head on one side. 'Soph, seriously. Isn't that kind of obvious?'

'Um, no?'

'You're you,' he says. 'Just bake.'

Well, DUH. Why didn't I think of that before?

The biggest bake sale in the history of Sunnystream. It really IS obvious. Flour and sugar and milk and eggs – none of those things are expensive. I have most of the cake-decorating stuff already. I'm grinning as I open Belle's front door. And then I remember what's on the front page of the paper and I'm grinning even more.

In the living room, Belle and Lola are throwing Maltesers into each other's mouths. Or trying to.

'Oh – I thought you guys had gone home,' says Belle, who's already dressed.

'Nope. I've got stuff for waffles. And you've GOT to read this headline!' I chuck her the paper. 'Wait, what do you mean, "you guys"?'

'You guys as in you and Maisie,' says Belle, catching the paper but not looking at it.

'Isn't she here?' I ask. 'She was here when I left. She was in the bathroom – the door was closed. Anyway, I was on the way home from –'

'It's always closed,' Belle interrupts. 'It just swings shut.'

'Oh,' I say. 'Well, maybe she got up early. Maybe she went to training after all.'

'Why would she do that?' says Belle, sounding a little worried. 'She said she was going to stay and help out at the clubhouse. We really need her today, or we won't get it all done.'

Belle's right – Maisie is the only one of us who can balance high enough on the ladder to paint the top half of the walls. If we can even get the money for the paint in time. 'I'm sure she won't be long.'

'Did she leave a note?' asks Belle.

'Not that I saw,' I say. 'I'll check.'

'And then we can have waffles, right?' says Lola as I go back up to the bedroom and shake out our sleeping bags. That's when I remember Gracie's whisper. Except it wasn't Gracie. Of course it wasn't. It was Maisie, going out somewhere.

And I bet I know where.

'I think she's gone to the clubhouse to do some balance work,' I tell the others. 'I think I heard her leave earlier. Shall we take her some waffles?'

'We don't have a waffle iron,' Belle says.

Of course! Why didn't I think of that?

Lola looks so devastated, it's actually funny.

'Well, why don't we get takeaway waffles at Sookie La La and bring them to her instead?' Belle says.

Thirty minutes later, we're crossing the park, going out of our minds trying not to eat the takeaway waffles before we get to Maisie. Mr Green gave them to us for free because he's proud of our campaign. How nice is that? The cinnamon sugar smells outrageously good. Belle is balancing four milkshakes like she's been training her whole life for this moment. Which she probably has – being prepared for a cafe job that she can do while she's studying at uni is probably in her ten-year plan. The milkshakes don't even have tops on them because #noplastic but she hasn't spilled a drop. It must be weird to be so perfect all the time. I wonder if it ever gets old.

'There!' I say, pointing at Maisie, across the park, where she's standing on the fence rail outside the clubhouse. She bends her knees, her arms out, and I know even from here that she'll have her concentrating-very-hard-right-now face on, which means she's going to do something tricky, like a flip combo. Shouldn't she have a mat for that, though?

She flings herself into the air and does one back handspring. Then another. It's like watching a firework arcing across the sky. I wonder, for the zillionth time, if one day I might actually be there at the Olympics, cheering her name till my voice is sore and scratchy.

Now it's the backflip, which is basically a whole backwards somersault in the air. She launches herself off the rail. 'Watch!' I say. 'This is what she's been practising.'

Maisie flicks around so fast, it's like she's being fast-forwarded. Truly, it's magical.

But at the last minute, as she lands, her feet slip.

Her stomach slams into the fence rail so hard, I swear I can hear it. We all gasp. She drops to one side and smacks into the ground. I can't believe it. Maisie never falls.

'MAISIE!' we scream, breaking into the fastest sprint of our lives. 'MAISIE.'

CHAPTER 13

When we get to Maisie, she's lying on her tummy on the ground, not moving. I have never seen her so still.

I freeze. I can't say anything. I can't do anything. My head starts to pound and I swallow, hard.

Belle turns Maisie onto her side and shoves her ear right up to Maisie's mouth to hear if she's breathing. 'She's alive.' She tilts her head back, opens up her mouth. And sticks in a finger. 'Let me just check if her airway is – ARGH! She bit me!'

'Stop being so loud,' Maisie mumbles.

'OMG,' says Lola, looking as relieved as I feel. 'Thank the sweet –'

'What's your name?' Belle asks gently as we all crowd around her. 'Can you tell me your name?'

'Bart Strabonsky,' Maisie says. Then she grins, and it's half a grimace, half a grin, but that's when I know she's OK. I can breathe again.

'Oh, Maisie,' I say. 'I thought … I thought you …' I shake my head.

'You thought I was a poo emoji?'

'Maisie, be serious. I'm trying to see if you're concussed. How old are you?' asks Belle.

'How old are *you*?' says Maisie, sitting up and rubbing her side.

'Is that sore? You might have cracked a rib,' says Belle. 'Does it hurt when you breathe?'

'Seriously, I'm fine,' says Maisie, though I know her well enough to know that she's trying not to show she's hurting. 'Just winded. I wanted to get this out of the way so I could definitely stay for the painting.'

'Dude, you could have died,' says Lola, sounding shaky. 'That was really scary. Don't do that again, OK?' There are tears in her eyes, and Lola *never* cries. She seems so strong and so sure of everything that it's weird to think of her being afraid.

'We brought you waffles,' I say, sitting down next to her. 'With cinnamon sugar.'

'And milkshakes,' says Belle, pulling out the caramel one from the cardboard tray, though how she didn't spill them when we were running is a genuine miracle.

As Maisie takes her milkshake, I notice her hands are trembling a little. 'Guys, maybe let's go inside,' I suggest. 'It's chilly out here.'

It takes Maisie ages to stand up, but once she's walking, she seems OK.

We sit on the (still not polished) floor of the clubhouse and suck down our (strawless) milkshakes, watching the time-lapse video of us fixing up the clubhouse on Lola's phone. Seeing what the clubhouse looked like at the start makes us realise how far it's come. Everything's there – Togsley sleeping in a corner (many times), Tally hanging upside down to sing the protest song, and all of us working SUPER hard. When it ends, my heart basically explodes with happiness and our cheers ring out like sports-teacher whistles because, truly, the acoustics in this place are amazing.

And sure, we haven't painted it properly, and the door is STILL hanging off its hinge, and Lola just pointed out a hole in the ceiling. But we've still got the whole weekend, right? It's only Friday. And maybe it's relief that Maisie is OK, or the thought of having somewhere to go at lunch next term, or maybe – and this is going to sound cheesy – it's because I wrote down those four words last night. Maybe it's because of what's in the newspaper – HANG ON! THE NEWSPAPER! ARGH!

'Belle, did you bring that paper?' I say. 'You guys are NEVER going to believe what's in it!'

She rummages in her bag and pulls out the *Sunnystream Gazette*.

'*SHARK TANK TO EMPTY*,' she reads. '*Sunnystream's giant entertainment hub and council building, The Shark Tank, has been closed indefinitely today.* OMG! What?'

I grab it off her. '*The emergency shut-down has occurred because it was discovered that the construction materials used may be poisonous. "We suspect there are toxic chemicals in the roof," said Sunnystream building inspector, Mr Steve Morrison, "and lead in the pipes."*'

I secretly love reading out loud. Sometimes I wonder if, deep down, I'm a bit of a show-off. '*"This type of thing can happen when the person in charge is trying to save money and brings in supplies from other countries where the rules aren't as strict," he went on. "It can happen when the person in charge is trying to bend the rules and hopes nobody notices. Luckily someone did and we're just in time. These sorts of things can make people very sick."*'

'The once-in-a-lifetime Japanese pancake competition, which was to be held at the Shark Tank on Monday morning, has been cancelled.'

We all squeal and high-five – except Maisie, who doesn't seem to want us to touch her.

'This is the best thing to ever happen to us!' Belle says, snatching back the paper. 'I mean, not the dangerous chemicals thing, obviously. But now people are going to need the clubhouse even more. Where else are they going to hold all the things that were supposed to be in the hall? And they're going to trust Mayor Magnus even less.' But then she reads a bit more of the article and frowns.

'What?' asks Lola.

'When asked whether this would halt the proposed demolition of the historic Corner Park Clubhouse, Sunnystream Mayor Mark Magnus said, "Stupid question. If you think this is going to stop me from bulldozing that dump, you have a pea for a brain."'

Oh.

'Does that mean he's just going to be angrier now?' Maisie asks quietly.

'Probably,' says Lola.

'Definitely,' says Belle.

Jeepers. Today is a real rollercoaster.

'Is that all it says?' I ask.

'There's one last bit,' says Belle. '*A community action group has planned a rally to protest its destruction on Monday at 10am. It is rumoured there will be a guest appearance by local celebrity YouTuber, Tally Powell.*'

'That's us!' Maisie and I say at exactly the same time. And then, 'Jinx!'

'Right,' says Belle. 'We need to refocus. Ideas for getting the paint money: I could tell the Eco Worriers to pick up coins on the pavements.' She's scribbling furiously in her notebook. 'That's a start. And maybe they could go over to Cloud Town and fine people who are using plastic bags. I could ask my friend Matilda if her mum –'

'Actually,' I begin, 'about the fundraising, I ran into Patrick and he thought –'

'You're allowed to use plastic bags in Cloud Town, Belle,' Lola interrupts. 'And the Eco Worriers aren't the police.'

'I never said –'

'Hate to break it to you,' Lola goes on, 'but you don't actually make the law. Besides, we'll need more than a couple of coins.'

As Belle crosses her arms, the wind picks up outside, and we feel it whip through the still-broken window. Maisie widens her eyes at me and I know what she's thinking: Lola's being snippy because the paper mentioned Tally and not her. It must be weird having a sister who's so famous. I feel sorry for her, but part of me also wants to say, *Hey, at least you have a sister.*

'What Patrick thought –' I try to say.

'I know *that*,' Belle says to Lola. 'We're just brainstorming. No idea is a bad idea.'

'And can you shut up about Matilda?' says Lola. 'I am so freaking sick of that girl.'

'If you met her, you'd love her. Everybody does. She sort of reminds me of you, actually.'

That is the worst possible thing Belle could have said. If there's one thing Lola hates, it's being like anyone else. You know those people?

'Umm,' says Maisie quickly, before Lola can snap back at Belle, 'we could have an auction for all the local businesses? The highest bidder gets to have Lola paint a mural on the side of their building.'

For an idea on the fly, I think that's pretty impressive. I give her a sneaky thumbs-up. She rubs her side. I knew it! She actually is hurt.

'Or we could –' I start, yet again.

'Nup,' says Lola curtly, picking up her phone. 'I don't do those anymore.'

'Why not?' I ask.

'I'm over them. So much effort.'

Maisie raises her eyebrows at Lola. If anyone knows about effort, it's her.

'Don't judge, Maisie!' says Lola. 'Sophia doesn't do heaps of stuff anymore and you don't hassle *her*.'

There's silence.

Because she's right.

I used to do almost as many activities as Belle. The Ukulele Ladies. Debating. Ballet. Girl Guides. Tennis. Diving. Swim Squad. I used to rush around town, different uniforms and instruments in different bags, changing on the run, a zillion reminders scribbled on my hands. I used to love craft. My hair was always full of glitter or baking flour, or was stiff with chlorine from the pool. I used to chat all the time. Like a football commentator, Gracie used to complain. People always thought I was so sunny. But now nobody knows what to say to me, and I don't know how to talk about Gracie, but I don't know how to *not* talk about her either, so being around people is stressful. I just want to hide away with my sadness, holding it close to me. This is probably going to sound weird, but the ache in my heart makes me feel as if she isn't quite gone, and I don't want anyone to try to take that ache away.

'I *cannot* believe you just said that,' Belle says quietly. 'Who even are you? Soph doesn't do those things because her twin –'

I cover my ears with my hands so I don't have to hear that last word. I say 'LA LA LA LA' really loudly, my eyes squeezed tight. When I open them again, she's saying '… be here if you don't want to. No-one's forcing you to take part.'

'Oh sure,' says Lola, 'so as soon as I leave you can invite Matilda to take my place? I don't think so.'

'What's Matilda even got to do with this?! You're just jealous because she's –'

'Matilda, Matilda, Matilda,' says Lola in a squeaky voice, pretending she's Belle. 'She's all you ever talk about now and it's BORING. Oh – and another thing? I bet your boyfriend is imaginary. And also? Now you're at that school, you clearly think you're better than us because you're heaps more bossy, if that's even possible. I liked you heaps better before.'

Belle looks super shocked, as if Lola has just slapped her. She doesn't say anything, which has literally never happened before. Our group never fights. It's one of the things that make us different. Sometimes in primary school, I could see other girls looking over at us, like they wished they could join in. We weren't the super-popular girls or the really sporty girls or the crazy-smart girls – we were our own combination of all those things, like a great paper bag of mixed lollies you get from the corner shop, and we never, ever argued. Not like this.

Belle turns to us. 'Do you … do you guys think I've changed?'

Maisie looks from Lola to Belle and back again. She shrugs, like everything's too hard, and presses both hands against her ribs, closing her eyes. It starts to rain, and the hole in the roof drips. We all ignore it, pretending we don't see the puddle that's forming on the floor.

'As if you guys haven't made new friends too,' says Belle over the sound of the drops on the roof, more defensive now. 'That's what high school is for!'

I look down, feeling my cheeks heat up.

'Of course we've made new friends,' says Lola, 'but it's not like we're always boasting about them because their mum's famous or whatever.' She slurps her spearmint milkshake loudly.

Belle takes a sharp breath, like she's about to breathe out fire. Or give Lola a lecture. Or both. Her cheeks are as red as mine now.

'This is stupid,' says Maisie bluntly. 'I don't have

time for all this drama. I'm just here because I love the clubhouse. If you're going to be lame, I'm going back to Holiday Hell. SnapChat me if you ever make up.'

Belle shrugs. 'Yeah, well, maybe we're not going to make up. Maybe we've just grown apart.'

I can almost hear my heart snapping in two.

'I've read about this,' Belle goes on. 'Maybe we were friends when we were younger and we'll always have the memories, but we'll never be as close again. Maybe we're like … like a broken vase that can't be put back together.'

'You've *read* about this?' says Lola incredulously. 'What are you, a robot who can only learn things from the internet? Be a freaking human for once.'

'A robot, a snob, a dictator. You seem to think I'm pretty multi-faceted, *Magnolia*. Well, you want to know what you are? *You* are a vain, self-centred, empty-headed narcissist.'

'What's a nar-sissy?' Maisie whispers to me.

I'm not sure it's the time to go into it. Lola HATES it when people use her real name. I want to say something to stop this – anything – but the words are stuck in my throat.

'SHUT YOUR BOSSY MOUTH,' shouts Lola. 'Shut the FUDGE up. This friendship is OVER.' She stands up and throws her milkshake – throws it *hard*. It flies through the air, like it's in slow motion, and hits Belle right in the face. It drips off her and spreads onto the floor, like radioactive slime.

And as Lola leaves through the front door, I know it's not the only thing around here that's broken.

CHAPTER 14

'Sophia,' my mum barks as soon as she walks into the kitchen that evening. I'm surrounded by eight batches of cupcakes, all in various stages of cooked and not-cooked and can't-be-cooked-because-I've-run-out-of-patty-pans-and-weirdly-you-can-only-buy-them-in-Cloud-Town. Mum doesn't seem to notice the cupcakes. She only has ten minutes to change before Pilates Me-Hearties, which is an exercise class where the teacher dresses like a pirate. Her grief counsellor recommended it for relaxation, which my mum is no good at. 'Liam has brought something to my attention.'

Liam is her very dapper assistant at the real-estate business who I can't stand. Me and Gracie sometimes had to go and sit with him in Mum's office when we were waiting for her after school. Liam is always looking at Facebook but pretending he's working very hard. Either that or he's doing a quiz about which Disney princess he's most like. Me and Gracie looked up his internet search history once when he wasn't there and he'd done that quiz thirty-two times. He just graduated from business school last year but he dresses like he thinks he's a full-on businessman. He's also a very big gossip. He told mum about seeing Lola and Maisie skateboarding off the roof of the public toilets into the sandpit at the park. Lola got grounded for a month. We had to sneak her jars of pickles through her bedroom window.

'He's seen something about you on the internet,' she continues, looking for her drink bottle in the cupboard, still saying nothing about my baking fest. 'Something about a fundraiser. Lola's sister and a trapeze – no, a towel rail? I can't remember. It sounded inappropriate. Is that anything to do with you? You know how I feel about cyber safety.'

My mum is weird about the internet. I think she's paranoid that someone is putting nudie pics of me on there. It happened to a year-nine girl at my school. Her ex-boyfriend uploaded them after they broke up at Sunny Stream of Talent. She sang a rap song about another dude and he was really mad, so he did it as revenge. What a jerk. But Mum should know I would never let ANYONE take nudie pics of me. I don't even like getting changed in front of Maisie. One of Gracie's nicknames for me was Never Naked.

Anyway, I know it's good to be safe online, but my mum goes crazy if she thinks my name is absolutely anywhere on the whole internet, and everyone's name is somewhere. I don't want to get into this whole internet thing with her now. I'm tired from the sleepover, and worried about Maisie, and most of all I'm in shock that suddenly, out of nowhere, I no longer have a group. So I've decided to do the bake sale alone, because I can't think of what else to do with myself.

And truthfully? I'm really mad.

About so many things.

I'm mad about losing the clubhouse and losing my childhood and losing my sister. I'm mad about the talent show and not singing 'Edelweiss'. I'm mad that it was always me and Gracie, left alone. I'm mad that Gracie never seemed to mind but I did. I really minded, but I never said. And most of all, I'm mad at my friends for just giving up on our friendship – just like that! After practically our whole lives. I look at the cupcakes and imagine them flying through the air, smashing against the Tasmanian oak folding doors that my mum thinks turn our lounge room into a versatile living space.

But I don't actually throw them. If those guys aren't going to help me, I'm just going to do it myself. So many things have been ripped from my life these last few months. At least this is one I can try to get back.

'We're saving Corner Park Clubhouse,' I say bitterly. 'At least, we were.'

'From what?' she asks.

'You mean from who. Who else? Mayor Magnus. He's demolishing the clubhouse and he wants to turn it into apartments. The Muscle Tower or something. And then take over the whole park. He's already got the bulldozer waiting. Apparently there was a notice about it on Handkerchief Place, but nobody seems to care.'

Mum freezes, like this is literally the worst thing she's ever heard. 'But the park is a huge selling feature for the suburb. It's why people want to move here. That, and the –'

'Community atmosphere,' I finish, because I've heard it a squillion times.

'Precisely,' says Mum. 'I must admit I didn't see the notice about it. When is this happening?'

'Monday. If you're interested, we're putting on a rally to, like, protest against it. That's what the whole trapeze thing is about.' Will there still be a rally? I don't know. My head hurts. I can't think about that right now. I remember the green milkshake flying through the air like dragon vomit.

'What do you mean, you're having a rally?' she asks. 'Of course I'm interested. This has huge implications for the future of the suburb.'

'Me and Belle and Lola and Maisie are having the rally. We're going to try to stop Mayor Magnus tearing it down. But everyone's invited. If enough people turn up, well, maybe we can do something to save it.' I think she's going to tell me it's a stupid idea. When I say it out loud, it does sound kind of dumb. We're just kids. But we've got to try. At least, I will. Who knows about the others? One annoying thing about not having a phone is that I don't know if they're all group-chatting now, or if they're still not speaking to each other.

But Mum doesn't say any of those things. She looks at me intensely. 'You organised that yourselves?'

I nod. 'Mostly. We can't let the clubhouse be destroyed. There are too many memories there. And if those apartments go up, it's like, Sunnystream won't be Sunnystream anymore. I'm baking this stuff to raise money. For the repairs. It's pretty run down.'

I think she's going to tell me off for saying 'like' too much. But it's like she didn't even notice.

'That's incredible,' Mum says, still looking at me – right into my face. 'Well done, sweetheart. What time on Monday?'

'Ten,' I say. 'In the morning. I know you're probably working then. I guess heaps of people will be.'

She frowns and goes back to hunting for the water bottle, and I know she's weighing up whether she can afford to miss whatever work thing she's supposed to be doing. But as she pulls it out of the cupboard and starts filling it up, she says, 'I'll email my clients about Monday. And the members of my networking group. I'll be there.'

This feels like a parallel universe. I kind of don't believe it. I wonder if she really is a robot, like Gracie always suspected, and she's malfunctioning.

I clear my throat. 'Mum? Can you take me to Bake the World a Better Place? It closes at seven. I need patty pans.'

You probably don't think this is a big deal, but Bake the World a Better Place is in Cloud Town, and it's right near the hospital. Anywhere near the hospital is the last place Mum would ever want to be. I bet she still dreams about it, just like I do. I know that she often takes the long way to go to the city, on the freeway, so she doesn't have to drive past.

But she nods and says, 'I'll cancel Pilates Me-Hearties. Pass me my keys.'

'Do you want a cupcake for the road?' I ask her as I pick one for myself and then offer her the tray.

She looks at the cupcakes, and then she looks at me, and her eyes fill with tears. 'Red velvet,' she whispers.

I nod. 'With cream-cheese icing.'

Then she starts to cry – really cry, the way I do when I sit by myself in the tree house.

I put down the tray and wrap my arms around her. She sobs for what feels like ages, but I do not let her go.

CHAPTER 15

The next morning, I'm yawning as I set up my cupcakes in the gazebo at Handkerchief Place. Mum stayed up to help me ice them till past midnight, even though she has bootcamp at quarter past five on Saturday mornings. I chose the icing colours to match the high-up clubhouse windows that make the lovely pattern on the floorboards – raspberry and orange and lemon. Mum's icing is really neat.

It took until we were decorating our very last cupcakes for me to work up the courage to say what I had been wanting to ask her all night. It's what I've been worrying about this whole time. 'What if … what if Mayor Magnus tears down the clubhouse anyway? And we have to watch?'

Actually, that's not even what I wanted to say – not all of it. The rest was: 'Won't watching the bulldozer roll over the clubhouse feel like I'm losing Gracie all over again? What if my heart is already so broken it actually shatters, like glass? Will I still be alive? Why isn't it equal, how much each person's life hurts?'

Mum finished piping an orange rose and reached over the kitchen bench. She tilted up my chin so I had to look into her eyes. 'It might not feel like it now,' she said quietly, 'but what you've gone through with Grace has made your heart grow.'

My eyes welled up when she said Gracie's name, and hers did too. But she didn't stop speaking. 'If the clubhouse is lost, it will live on in that big, strong heart, and we can be grateful for the time we had with it. It hurts because we love,' she said, and it was like she'd read my mind in that spooky way mums sometimes do. 'It isn't fair, but that's the trade-off. And what would be the point of life if we all gave up loving?

'Your father and I,' she continued.

But I shook my head and closed my eyes.

'We love you,' she whispered. 'That's all I was going to say.'

I'm still thinking about that now as I finish setting up my music/cash box. When I'm done, I pick up my sign and walk over to Judy's Eye-Scream. 'Can you please take a picture of me with this? And put it on Instagram? I don't have a phone anymore,' I explain to Judy.

If Lola had been there to help me, the sign wouldn't be so lame. But she wasn't. So it is. I didn't plot it out beforehand, so the last three letters are all squished and the words slant upwards because I can't write straight without lines. I did it this morning, and the glitter paint isn't really dry yet.

Judy grabs her phone. 'Oh, Soph,' she says when I hold up the sign. 'That's beautiful.'

It says: *Bake Sale Saturday! Gracie's Favourites. Help Save Corner Park Clubhouse.*

She takes the photo and I try to smile, though when she lets me look at it, it's sort of a scared smile.

'Where's the gang?' she asks when we've posted.

I swallow. 'We're not a gang anymore. We had a huge fight. Belle thinks we've grown apart. So I guess it's over.'

Here's the thing I love about Judy. She doesn't say, 'Don't be ridiculous – you'll sort it out,' like a mum would. Like *my* mum did when we were icing the cupcakes. Judy says, 'That's tough, kid. Want to tell me about it?'

'Not really,' I say. 'We were trying to raise money, and then Maisie almost died, and Lola really lost her mind, though maybe that's kind of to do with Tally, and Belle has this new friend who's better than us.'

Judy snorts. 'Not possible. No-one's better than you g– wait! Did you say Killer almost *died*?'

'Kind of. She fell off the fence at the clubhouse doing beam practice. She's been skipping gym training to help us fix up the clubhouse in time for the rally,' I add. 'But we don't even have enough money to finish painting it. If anyone shows up on Monday, they're probably going to think it's a dump that deserves to be knocked down.'

Judy frowns. 'Doesn't have to be perfect. You've cleared out the junk, right? And Mikie fixed up the steps?'

I nod. 'And we cleaned, like, heaps. And we did the undercoat. Well, some of it. But there are still holes in the floor. And the ceiling. The door needs fixing. So do the windows. And we can't afford any of that. What else are we supposed to do?'

'Kid, sometimes you've just got to let people in,' she says. 'Sometimes you've just gotta ask for help.'

As I walk back over to the gazebo, I think about that. I wonder if she was only talking about the clubhouse, or if she's been watching me since the summer.

Lola would be impressed with my Instagram marketing. Within five minutes, I'm swamped. One lady buys seven cupcakes for her granddaughter's seventh birthday. Patrick swings by on his way to holiday baseball training and gets enough for his whole team. I baked 132 red-velvet cupcakes, but now I'm worried that might not be enough. Luckily Mr Green from Sookie La La drops off a peach pie for me to sell. 'That really was Gracie's favourite,' he says with a wink. And he's right.

Nobody else says anything about Gracie, even though her name is on the sign. And some of them still do the weird thing where they're not quite sure where to look. But some of them smile deep, and I know it's because of Gracie. Once when she was in hospital and no-one could visit – not even me – she Skyped assembly and waved to everyone on the big screen in the hall. The whole school cheered and stamped their feet and the principal couldn't stop them. Not for ages. Sometimes I used to wonder … Would they have cheered that long for me?

I'm just about to get the wishing feeling again when Maisie arrives, walking kind of slowly. She's brought a tray of rice bubble squares. She helps me handle the cash, which is coming thick and fast. I sell forty cupcakes – FORTY! – to the Friends of the Sunnystream Sidewalks, who weed the cracks between the pavement stones. The Eco Worriers come by on their way to help out customers at Buck's with the whole no-bag situation. I give them some half price. I sort of love those guys.

'Holy heckballs,' Maisie says as she flicks through the pile of money. 'We could paint the whole Shark Tank with all this.'

'How are your ribs feeling?' I ask between customers.

'Huh,' says Maisie, which is Maisie for 'I don't want to talk about it'. I keep watching her carefully, and I can tell she isn't feeling good.

When I have only eight cupcakes left, Lola arrives. She's carrying a plate of what I think might have been Anzacs, but they're black and crumbling, like discs of soot. She looks embarrassed. 'I sort of got distracted,' she says as she plonks them on the table. She has earrings on again! They're tiny red maple leaves. Oh my heart.

'Distracted by what a massive jerk you were yesterday?' says Maisie, grinning.

Eek! But you know what? Lola just grins back, and throws a burnt Anzac at her.

'Hey – careful. She's injured, remember?' says Belle, climbing up the steps to the gazebo.

Lola turns, and her smile turns into a glare. 'Hello, Isobelle,' she sneers.

'Hello, *Magnolia*,' says Belle, plonking down a plate of honey-joys with a sign on them that says they're sugar-free. How can honey be sugar-free?

'Seriously?' sighs Maisie, putting her hands on her ribs and frowning.

'Well, I –' says Lola.

'*She* –' says Belle.

They both start talking at once, and I feel as if something inside me is being crushed.

'If you think –' begins Lola.

'Your problem –' begins Belle.

Suddenly I just can't handle this anymore.

'SHUT. UP,' I yell. 'AND JUST LISTEN FOR ONCE.'

Everyone flinches. This really isn't like me.

'I don't care that we're all at different schools now. I don't care that we can only FaceTime for twelve minutes every second Thursday. I don't care if you have new friends or whatever.' (That bit's actually a lie. Oh well.) 'We've always been best friends and there is NO WAY that's changing. ZERO. So get used to it.'

People all around Handkerchief Place have turned to stare, but you know what? I DON'T CARE.

'The clubhouse needs us, and we need the clubhouse,' I continue. 'We're doing this thing TOGETHER, so start thinking about someone other than yourselves for a second. Start thinking about the memories we'll be saving and the people we could actually help if we got this thing going again.' Then I say something that even *I* find a bit shocking. 'If you're still hating on each other, whatever. I don't give a flying fudge. But stop for a second and think about me.' I swallow. 'Because you guys are all I have now.'

There's a big pause. I don't know what I'm expecting to happen, but it's definitely not my friends giving me a huge round of applause. Which is what happens next.

Maisie says, 'Bravo! Bravo!' and Belle wolf-whistles so loudly that the rest of us wince.

'Sorry, guys,' Lola says when the clapping stops. 'You're right – I was being a total brat. Like, worse than the Cloud Town Cougars. I don't know what got into me. I guess … I guess I'm finding high school harder than I thought.'

'If anyone should apologise, it's me,' says Belle, 'You're right – I *am* bossy. And I'm sorry that I talk about Matilda all the time. I've actually had some time for self-reflection …' She pulls out yet another notebook and flicks to a page where she's written a list under the heading 'Self-reflection'.

I expect Lola to roll her eyes, but she just raises an eyebrow and chews on a fingernail. I want to tell her to stop because she'll ruin her nail polish – it's clear with rainbow speckles and it reminds me of fairy bread – but I don't say anything.

Belle clears her throat and tucks her honey-blonde hair behind her ears. 'I've concluded that I think Matilda is so important to me because I never thought anyone would ever like me except for you guys, and that maybe … maybe we'd known each other so long that you didn't even really like me, you just didn't remember life without me. I know I'm a nerd, and stubborn, and a perfectionist. I never thought that anyone cool would ever want to be my friend. So, sorry about that.'

'Of course we like you,' says Maisie. 'You'd do anything to help anyone. Look what you did for the clubhouse. Look how you're always trying to find ways to help a dumbass like me.'

'You're not dumb!' I say. 'Don't say it. And Belle, you're perfect how you are. Not that you have to be perfect,' I add. 'You know what I mean.'

'I'm the dumb one,' Lola and Belle say at EXACTLY the same time. 'Jinx!' they yell, also at the same time. 'Shut up,' they say at the same time. And then we all laugh and go in for a group hug – all except Maisie, who hangs back. I can see from the way she's pursing her lips that she's in real pain now. Eek.

When we've finished with the hugging, I offer them all a cupcake.

'Soph!' says Lola, looking down at the cupcake and back up at me.

'They're red –' Belle begins, her eyes wide.

'Yeah,' I say, ducking my head and blushing a little. 'I know.'

'With cream-cheese icing,' says Maisie. 'I'm proud of you. Gracie would be, too.'

'I know,' I whisper. 'She would.'

While we wait for someone to come and buy the last four sweet treats, we take turns to frisbee the burnt Anzacs into the bin. Maisie is the best, obviously. Belle is the worst. Then we count up the money. We have enough to buy the paint. But is there such a thing as paint that dries, like, instantly?

My mum is our final customer. She comes by after showing the house on Tea Cake Crescent to that couple again. She says they're pretty close to buying and she wants to give them some cupcakes to sweeten the deal. She smiles at my friends – a real smile, not the fake one from her real-estate posters.

'Belle, Maisie, Lola,' she says as she pays. 'Nice to see you all getting along.' EMBARRASSING. Now they'll know I told her about the fight! Thanks for nothing, Mum.

But if they care, they're doing a good job not showing it.

'Thanks, Mrs H,' they say, and then they all say 'Jinx!' again. As we pull weird faces at each other, I know we're all thinking the same thing: the second F in BFFs is actually for real.

'A bunch of monkeys, you lot,' says Mum, putting away her purse. 'Come for a sleepover soon.'

'Wait – Mum, is there such a thing as paint that dries super fast?' I ask. This is exactly the kind of boring house-y question that my mum will know everything about. 'Really quickly, I mean,' I say, correcting my grammar. 'Like, will be dry by the end of tomorrow.'

Her whole face lights up. 'Internal or external paint? Walls or ceilings?'

'Internal walls,' says Belle enthusiastically. 'I've read that it needs to go through both a drying and hardening phase.'

'Exactly,' says Mum. 'Now, of the water-based paints, I'd recommend …'

This goes on between them for so long that Lola gets hungry and tries to nibble on one of the few remaining burnt Anzacs, which she has to spit out. 'Oh!' she says to me and Maisie. 'There's something I've been trying to remember since I woke up and it's just popped into my mind.'

'How long you have to wait till morning tea?' Maisie asks.

'How many boys you have a crush on?' I ask.

'No, stupid,' says Lola, grabbing me in a headlock and ruffling my hair. 'It's a word we learned in Art History last term. *Kintsugi*. It's a Japanese word. It's when something has a crack and when it's repaired, they paint that crack with gold, so that the broken bit becomes something beautiful.'

'*Kintsugi*,' I say. The broken bit becomes beautiful. I'm going to have to think some more about that.

'Speaking of broken,' says Maisie, looking kind of worried. 'Um, guys …' She winces. 'I know I'm supposed to paint the high bits in the clubhouse and I don't want to let you down, but … I kind of need to go home. To bed. This hurts so bad I'm gonna throw up.'

This is like hearing that Santa Claus is shaving off his beard – it's just wrong. Maisie never complains about anything. Even my mum looks worried.

'Sweetheart,' she says to Maisie, 'I think you might need a doctor. Let me take you home.'

CHAPTER 16

On Sunday morning, Belle and Lola and I walk gloomily through the clubhouse, looking at all the things that still need to be done and wishing Maisie was with us. We only have one day left to cram in the rest of Steps 3, 4 and 5 – TODAY! Mikie took us to the Hard Hair Store yesterday afternoon and we got the rest of the undercoat, and the water-based quick-drying wall paint that Mum recommended. Because of the bake sale, we even had money for floor polish, and for black fabric for new stage curtains, and to get more flyers printed.

But the door is still broken, the windows too. We haven't figured out how to get the stage curtains down. The garden is full of weeds and leaves. Now we have the money, but we're not going to have enough time to get it all done. Last night we tried to finish the top half of the undercoat, but without Maisie, we only got two walls done because we're really scared to be up the ladder, and that slows us down. The other two walls are still dirty-tooth brown. The whole place looks …

'Disgusting,' says Belle gloomily as we lie down on the stage and look up at the tatty curtains. We should really keep painting, but it all just seems too hard. 'And after everything we've done, too.'

'A dump,' Lola agrees. 'Even if people show up for the rally, they're gonna take one look at this and think we're a joke. We'll never get this finished by tomorrow. Not without, like, an army of robots.'

'At some point in the near future, robots will probably do most of the jobs that humans do now,' says Belle. 'So most people won't have jobs anymore and the main challenge is going to be …'

She gets even more intense when she's feeling stressed and I can sense a real robot rant coming on, which is going to make Lola crazy. So as soon as she pauses for breath, I jump in and say, 'At least Maisie's OK.'

We FaceTimed her last night, and I don't know how, but Belle was one hundred per cent right about

Maisie's injury. Mrs Zhang took Maisie to the doctor and it turns out she cracked two ribs when she slipped off the fence rail. One of them has a jaggedy edge and that's what was giving her the weird pain. It could have punctured her lung.

'The treatment for broken ribs is just to rest,' she told us. 'Boring.'

'So you don't get a cast?' Lola asked. 'I've always wanted a cast.'

'What did your parents say?' said Belle.

'They, um, well,' said Maisie, 'they said they didn't want me going to the clubhouse again. Like, ever.'

'WHAT?!' we yelled.

'But hang on, hang on – it's fine because Soph's mum was really good with them.'

The Zhangs had wanted to know why Maisie was doing something so dangerous and why she hadn't been attending training when they'd paid for it – paid *heaps* for it – which they said they're never going to do again. No more gym – like, ever. (Eek.)

But then apparently my mum explained to them about the clubhouse and how we are actually trying to help. She said that we're a group with a social conscience and strong core values and she even told them how good Maisie is at coding. Go Mum!

The FaceTime on Mum's laptop froze after she told us that bit, so I missed the end of the conversation. 'Did she say anything else?' I ask.

'Yeah, they're gonna let her come over today if she's feeling well enough, and if she promises to sit very still and do nothing,' says Lola.

'I literally cannot imagine Maisie sitting still,' I say, watching the breeze from the broken window move through the curtains in a wave. 'She's such a fidget.'

'Am not,' comes a voice from the doorway.

We scramble up to see her standing there, grinning, holding a tray of waffles from Mr Green at Sookie La La that smell like HEAVEN. I feel relief slush through me like a caramel milkshake. As we run over, it's so hard not to hug her to Tuesday and back, but you really can't hug someone with broken ribs.

'Maisie,' I say, as she hands out the waffles and we sit on the steps, 'are you OK? About gym, I mean.'

'You mean having to quit? Never going to happen. I'm going to wait till my ribs have healed, and then I'm going to talk to my parents about it again.'

Isn't that totally incredible? If that was me, I'd be feeling super sorry for myself, moping. Not Maisie.

'Shouldn't you guys be painting instead of just lounging around?' she asks in between mouthfuls.

We groan, and fill her in on everything we still have to do. Which is a lot.

'That's not technically possible,' she points out. 'I feel so bad that I can't help. That was super dumb, what I did.'

'It wasn't,' Lola says loyally. 'But I guess we just … we just aimed a little too high. We're only kids, after all.'

'We're *so much* more than that,' says Belle. 'But even if we work all night, this will never be done by tomorrow. What else can we do?'

That's exactly what I asked Judy at the gazebo yesterday. I think back to what she said to me. And you know what? It makes sense. 'I know we like to do things ourselves. I know that we're strong, entrepreneurial businesswomen,' I say, glancing at Belle, who nods approvingly. 'But maybe … maybe it's time to ask for help. Loles?' I ask. 'Could I borrow your phone?'

I take it and walk towards the red Japanese maple, punching in the number. It was the very first number Gracie and I learned by heart. 'Good work,' my dad told us that day. 'Now, if there's ever an emergency, you get someone to call me, OK?'

We're about to lose Corner Park Clubhouse and that's definitely an emergency. I take a deep breath.

I make the call.

CHAPTER 17

Turns out Judy was right. Sometimes you've just got to ask.

Punk Sherman is here because Belle was brave enough to ask him to come, even though she has a rule not to let her mum's boyfriends into her life. He's up his long ladder, fixing the holes in the roof, and Francine is up another ladder, painting the tricky high bits. The Eco Worriers are doing the low bits. Belle called them too, and you can tell they feel super important to be involved. It's really cute. Because of the super-duper fast-drying paint, it looks like maybe, just maybe, we're going to get it all done in time.

Lola asked her whole family, though she made

Tally promise to look after Gwynnie and Pop so they don't wreck anything. They're all out working in the garden now with Mrs Powell. Mr Powell has brought over a sewing machine and he and Lola's Aunt Claire are making the new curtains. Lola was giving them a hand for a while but she keeps disappearing right when I want to ask her things. Rishi brought the whole of RexRoy with him, and they're investigating how to fix the windows.

Even though Maisie really didn't want to, she called Coach Jack and asked him to bring over his drill and fix the door. And just like she predicted, he was furious that she was doing those flips on the fence rail with no safety mat. He took her outside and gave her a lecture about trust that went for ages (eek). But now he's helping Judy and me to put the bottom hinge back on the door and sand the side so it actually shuts. Coach Jack and Judy work so well as a team that Mikie starts looking jealous. Maybe that's why he walks into Punk Sherman's ladder and cuts his head. When the blood's gushing out, it gets in his eyes and he accidentally kicks the last tin of paint all over the floor. It takes me and Belle the rest of the morning to clean it up.

In case you're wondering, my dad's phone went straight to voicemail. Maybe he was on the plane to

Los Angeles or something, but it was so nice to hear his voice again. It's deep and warm and clear. Like a newsreader's voice, Gracie always used to say. Like a handsome weatherman.

I was going to call Mum, but then I remembered that on Sunday mornings she's at Ice-Cycle, which is an indoor cycling class that's held in a giant fridge. It's for people who hate sweating, which is totally my mum.

So I called Mikie and Judy and Patrick instead.

'Are the posters finished?' asks Maisie when we stop for an iced tea, which Mrs Powell brought in a giant thermos.

'Lola's got them,' says Belle. 'Where is she? We're getting the Eco Worriers to put them around town at six tomorrow morning.'

Yesterday afternoon, Lola took a picture of Togsley on the clubhouse stairs looking really pleading and made it into a poster. It says, 'If you give a pug about Sunnystream, be at the Corner Park Clubhouse at 10am MONDAY.' She's put the picture all over social media. Rishi and his band put it all over theirs, and wrote a song that they're going to play at the rally.

Speaking of songs, earlier today Tally sang *Somewhere Over the Rainbow* on the ukulele in a final plea to get her followers to sign her online petition. A famous actress shared it on her Facebook account and it went viral. That famous actress was one of Matilda's mums.

'Mayor Magnus is going down,' says Belle with glee before she gulps the last of her iced tea.

I think about Mayor Magnus as we get back to work. I think about why he might be like he is. 'A bully was often bullied,' my dad used to say. Did someone bully Mayor Magnus when he was a kid? I wonder if he ever came to Corner Park Clubhouse. If he played here with his friends. If he even had friends. If he was lonely, like I was last term. If he felt sore in his heart, and ashamed.

And then, even though I try not to, I start thinking about not seeing my friends every day when school is back. I think about that as Coach Jack drives me and Maisie to the Hard Hair Store in his ute so we can hire a floor polisher, listening to RexRoy's last album with the windows down.

By the time we get back, it's late afternoon. Judy has to go to her shop to get ready for the after-dinner crowd. Gwynnie and Pop are getting cranky and the Powells take them home. RexRoy have to rehearse their rally song.

Patrick needs to be back home in time for dinner. 'Thanks for inviting me,' he says. His cheeks are apple-pink and he looks cheerful, just like his old self. 'Will you get it all done, do you reckon?' He looks at the patchy floors, which we haven't started polishing yet, and the one wall that still needs another coat of paint.

'We'll do it,' I say confidently. 'Even if it takes us all night, we'll do it. See you tomorrow?'

'Tomorrow,' he says.

I can't believe it – tomorrow! I'm so nervous I want to do cartwheels. I can't imagine what Maisie must be feeling, having to sit there so still. But Judy brought us over a badge machine, and now Maisie's thinking that maybe we can make badges for people to wear at the rally. At first we don't know what to put on them.

'Togsley again?' she suggests.

'I don't want to saturate our brand with just one image,' says Lola, appearing from nowhere with black paint up her arm. 'I want people to think we have a constant stream of fresh ideas.'

Belle looks very impressed with this logic. 'You're a mean marketing unit, Powell,' she says happily. 'Anyone got any other ideas?'

And I do.

'Are you sure?' Maisie says quietly when I finish explaining. 'You're OK with this?'

'Oh, it's *so* good,' Lola says, bouncing on her toes.

'If you're ready,' says Belle, 'that would be awesome. No pressure.'

I'm definitely ready. 'We need yellow fairy floss and fishing line. Can one of you guys get those? Buck's will have them.'

I run home, which is empty, of course. On Sunday evenings Mum has her Yoga in a Toga class. I ruffle Togsley's ears and apologise for leaving him alone so long. I feed him quickly, and then I run into Mum and Dad's bedroom. It feels kind of naughty to be there – kind of weird. I go over to the wardrobe on Dad's side, expecting it to be empty. I thought all his stuff would be in the city apartment now. But it's full. Suits and shirts and jeans. A jacket he bought with patches on the elbows that Mum thought was too shabby. It smells like him – aftershave and drycleaning. And there, hanging over a coathanger, are approximately eighty-three shiny ties. I know because Gracie and I counted them once on a boring rainy afternoon, peeling them off one by one and throwing them in a big pile.

I weave my fingers through their soft, silky tongues, looking for the one I remember him wearing at our year six graduation party. There's a photo of him and me that night. He got it printed at Officeworks to put in a frame for his office, he liked it so much. I see the tie with the tiny shooting stars that he wore to Gracie's baseball presentation night because her team was called the Comets. I see the one he bought in London when he took us away with him for Aunty Katie's wedding and we left Mum behind to do a big auction. We helped him choose the pattern – little red double-decker buses being driven by mice.

Just when I start to feel like I can't breathe, there it is. I grab it and slam the door and sprint back to the park. And there she is. Lemon Tart. Maisie holds her leash out to me. I take it and bend down to pick up Gracie's rabbit. She's so warm and familiar in my hands, like I'm holding a packet of heated-up love.

Ten minutes later, Lola has chopped the sparkly purple tie down the middle and opened it up so it fits round Lemon Tart's neck like a cape. It's a little small, but it will have to do. Belle has bought the fairy floss from Buck's and figured out how to tie it on to the top of Lemon Tart's head with the fishing line to look like clown wig hair. I fold a little origami cap and Lola copies the Mega Mayor logo onto it *exactly*. We sit Lemon Tart up on her hind legs so her tummy pokes out.

'She is *ridiculously* patient,' Lola says, marvelling at how Lemon Tart just sits there and lets you do whatever.

'You're telling me. Once me and …' But Gracie's name catches in my throat. I shake my head. Maisie squeezes my arm.

Lola winks at me. 'Lights, camera, action,' she says.

An hour later, Maisie's dad has picked up Lemon Tart and Tally has done our printing, and we have two hundred badges of that sweet, fat rabbit looking amazingly like Mayor Magnus. The words SOMETIMES BIGGER ISN'T BETTER circle the edge. We pin them on each other and just stand there, tired but determined, smiling like idiots.

'I wouldn't normally condone using our clubhouse funds for leisure activities,' says Belle when we've done a selfie, 'but just this once, do you want to get pre-dinner Judy's?'

'One more thing,' Lola says. 'Come check this out.'

We open up the black stage curtains that Punk hung up for us. At the back of the stage, along the whole wall, she's painted the word *KINTSUGI* really big in black running writing with little rivers of gold running through each letter. It looks beautiful. 'That's for you, Killer,' she says. 'Remember? The broken bit is beautiful.'

'My ribs are totally *kintsugi*,' says Maisie.

And maybe my heart is too.

CHAPTER 18

Up at Handkerchief Place, there's a cold wind blowing, but the fairy lights are twinkling on the gazebo and everything feels golden and precious.

Judy's new flavour of the week is SubLIME and Coconut Bliss, so things with Mikie must be going pretty well. 'And I've made one as a tribute to you guys,' she says. No way! 'It's called Rum and Raisin' Hell. Do you want …' I can tell she's about to offer us a sample but she doesn't want Belle to see she's using those little plastic spoons. 'Do you want me to help out with anything at the rally tomorrow?' she says instead.

'You could hand out badges?' I say, pulling one out of my bag to show her.

Judy doesn't laugh very often. She's kind of intense. But when she sees Lemon Tart Magnus, she actually has to lean on the counter, she's laughing so hard. When she recovers she says, 'It would be an honour.'

I get Rum and Raisin' Hell and Belle gets Honey, Comb Your Hair, and the others get the lime one, and we sit out in the cool starlight on the grass, not saying anything at all. I guess we're all thinking about what's going to happen at ten o'clock tomorrow. If we can make a difference. If little can beat big. When we finish our ice-creams, we lie down and look up at the moon, our heads all together like four points of a star.

'Will Mayor Magnus even show up?' Maisie asks eventually. 'Or will it just be the guy driving the bulldozer?' She shudders and we all wince. Poor Corner Park Clubhouse.

'Oh, he'll show,' Belle says spitefully. 'He can't keep away from a crowd. He loves the attention.'

'Will anyone else show up?' asks Lola. 'Aside from our families?'

'I don't even know if my mum is coming,' I say. 'She says she is, but she'll probably get an urgent work call at the last minute, I just bet. I guess Monday's a tricky day for everyone.'

'She'll come,' says Maisie.

'You can share my mum,' says Lola. 'She basically wants to adopt you already.'

'Does your dad know about it?' Belle asks me. She's always weirdly fascinated by other people's dads.

'No,' I sigh. 'I don't think he's coming back …' I think about his shirts in the cupboard. The whole thing's confusing. 'I don't know. Guys? I just want to say …'

I start to feel my throat closing up, my words being swallowed down again. But then I think about Gracie, and about living a big, brave life. I close my eyes, thankful for the velvety darkness, and try again.

'Whatever happens tomorrow,' I say, 'even if nobody shows up, even if the clubhouse gets torn down … I'm proud that you're my friends. And I'm sorry I haven't been that good at keeping in touch this year. I really miss you. Like, *really*.'

'OMG, that's just what I was thinking!' says Lola at the same time as Maisie says, 'Me too,' and Belle says, 'TOTALLY.'

'*I may not always be there with you, but I'll always be there for you*,' says Lola. 'That's not Shakespeare,' she adds. 'It's Instagram.'

'It's still nice,' I say loyally.

'Hey – Soph!' calls Judy across the square. 'Stand up for a second.'

I scramble up and she yells, 'Catch!'

Two boxes come flying towards me. Ball sports are not my forte, but somehow I catch them both – one in each hand. Gracie would be proud. Actually, she'd be amazed.

The long thin one is sparklers. The short fat one is matches. We all huddle in as we light them so the breeze doesn't blow the spark away.

As each one catches light, there's that exciting fizz, and then we're all holding them, twirling them against the sky.

'Quick – what should we write? Before they go out!' says Maisie.

'Corner Park Clubhouse,' says Belle.

'Too long!' says Lola as they sizzle closer to our fingers.

'Then just CPC,' I say.

CPC, we scrawl in the air, faster and faster, till it's blazing across the sky.

'That's us,' says Maisie happily when the last sparkler's finished and Belle's put all the rubbish in the bin. 'The Corner Park Club.'

Without anyone saying anything else, we put our arms around each other in a circle, like we've been doing since we were eight. Our arms are longer now, but our hearts are the same. Or perhaps they are bigger, too, with everything we've been through together.

'To the CPC,' Belle says.

'To the CPC,' we say together.

'And to *kintsugi*,' I whisper. But I don't think anyone hears.

Then it starts to spit with rain – just lightly at first, but then harder. Maisie can't run, so we walk with her, but by the time we make it back across the oval to the clubhouse, we're all drenched. We all call home and soon our parents arrive with dry clothes and snacks.

'Is it OK if I stay really late?' I ask Mum as she hands over a unicorn onesie that I sometimes wear as pyjamas. 'We haven't even started the floor yet.' (We got kind of distracted with the badges, truth be told.)

But Mum doesn't answer. She's looking around the clubhouse in wonder. She's looking at the stage, and I know what she's seeing: Gracie walking across it, her curls bouncing, to get another certificate, another trophy.

Mum turns to me, her face shining with pride. 'Sophia, this is an exceptional renovation – and in such a short time too. I couldn't be more impressed. If you need to, you can stay out all night.'

And that's just what we do.

By the time we finish the painting, it's already past our bedtime. And then we have to get down on our hands and knees and put the polish on the floor. We go over the polish with the machine, which is loud and heavy, and then we chase each other around in our socks to give the floor a final bit of sparkle. Maisie sits on the stage and points out bits we've missed. She totally gets into it and by the end, she's being bossier than Belle.

'Not a bad effort,' she says when we're so tired we plonk ourselves down on a pile of the old stage curtains. It must be after midnight. Everything in my body feels sore – even more sore than the holidays I did Ballet Bootcamp at Miss Claudine's in Cloud Town before my dance exam.

'What do you mean, "not bad". It's perfect!' says Belle indignantly. 'Now, all we have left to do is –'

But we don't hear what she says next, because hail starts to fall and it clatters on the roof so loudly we have to cover our ears. When it finally stops, none of us can get up. We're too tired.

'We can finish the rest off in the morning,' says Belle. 'I'll set my phone alarm for seven.'

'Nine!' says Lola.

'Eight-thirty,' I say, burrowing into the curtains and pulling them over my head.

The wind blows all night, making a tree whip against the side of the clubhouse. It feels like I'm awake at two o'clock and three o'clock and four o'clock, wondering what it all means. If it's like this in the morning, nobody will come to the protest. But then again maybe you can't bulldoze a building in the rain, and that means Mayor Magnus will stay away too, and Corner Park Clubhouse will survive another day.

Then I worry that even if it's sunny nobody will come. I worry that people will be too busy working. I worry that we've left it too late – that we should have noticed what was happening to Sunnystream sooner. I worry that nobody cares like we do. I wish I had my phone so I could google 'does a bulldozer work in the rain'. I want to snuggle in close to Maisie, but I don't want to hurt her. I wish I was in Gracie's bed, where I'd often end up on stormy nights. It must be nearly sunrise by the time I drift off to sleep. Maybe the Eco Worriers are already up, putting rally posters round town.

When Belle's alarm goes off at eight-thirty, we can barely open our eyes.

'Did any of you get any sleep?' I ask. 'That storm was crazy.'

'Belle sure did,' says Lola. 'She snored in my ear all night.'

'Did not!' says Belle. 'I don't *snore.*'

'How would you even know?' says Lola. 'I filmed you, anyway. Check it out.' She throws Belle her phone, which Belle misses. Practising ball skills is not one of Belle's top one hundred life priorities.

'That's a violation of privacy! That's a literal crime!'

'It's a crime how much you sound like a popcorn machine,' says Lola. 'Seriously – listen.'

The others crowd around the phone as I crawl up out of the curtain nest and throw open the (fully functioning!) door.

Oh no.

'Guys! Get out here!' I call as I take it all in.

The sky is blue. There's not a puff of wind. And the garden looks like it's been attacked by a gang of mutant trolls. There are leaves and bark everywhere, a broken branch, dirt on all the paths between the flower beds. The lavender looks as if it's been stomped on. The red Japanese maple has lost half its leaves and it looks embarrassed, like someone stole its undies while it was at swimming lessons. Some of the little tiles from Lola's mosaic have come off the sundial. One of the drainpipes is half hanging off the side of the clubhouse.

'It's a disaster zone,' says Lola flatly. 'How long till people start arriving?'

'An hour and a half,' Belle says, checking her watch. 'Actually, one hour and twenty-three minutes.'

'We can do this,' I say, trying to sound more confident than I feel. 'Remember what Winston Churchill said?' To tell the truth, I can't exactly remember but I'm sure Belle does.

'This is no time for quotes,' she says. 'This is time for action. Someone get some garbage bags.'

We work in a panic, crazy fast and super efficient. We stuff leaves in the bags and sweep up the soil. We tie the drainpipe to the building with Lola's hair ribbons. We pick up the tiles and puff up the lavender. We're hungry and tired. We sweat. A lot.

And just when we're finished and ready to get some yoghurt from Buck's for breakfast, Lola looks at her phone and says, 'We can't. It's ten o'clock. People will be here any second.'

My tummy growls, but suddenly I'm too nervous to think about food. I'm excited, and proud, and impatient, like I've mixed a weird potion in my stomach. I look at us, red-faced and dirt-smeared in our weird brought-from-home clothes – Maisie in her skeleton onesie, and Belle in her mum's psychedelic aerobics leggings, and Lola in Rishi's old RexRoy band T-shirt and Tally's plaid pyjama bottoms. I can't help but smile.

'We look …' I don't have the words.

'Dedicated to the cause,' Belle finishes.

'Like loons,' says Maisie.

'Original,' says Lola.

After that, we don't say anything at all. Because now it's five past ten.

And ten past ten.

And quarter past ten.

And nobody – *nobody* – shows up.

CHAPTER 19

Mayor Magnus isn't here, which I guess is a good thing. But no-one else is either. The sun might be out, but it's gloomy as we sit on the steps and wait.

'Where *is* everyone?' Belle asks for the millionth time – the zillionth.

'Maybe the town has been taken over by aliens,' says Maisie, who is very interested in the possibility of life on another planet. 'Maybe we're the only humans left who haven't been beamed up into their spaceship. That would be a bummer, by the way. I would hate to miss that.'

'I wouldn't,' I say, and shiver. I'm scared of aliens and I don't *love* heights. It's twenty past ten and now there's literally nothing else we can do to fix the clubhouse – not a window to shine, not a stray leaf or a patch of grime anywhere. The clubhouse is finished and smells like beeswax and fresh paint. Steps 1 to 5 are over.

As I look up at the little row of windows in their sweet candy colours, I think, *If it's your last day standing, Corner Park Clubhouse, at least you look your best.* I think about last days and goodbyes and Gracie's baseball uniform – dark blue with white stars bursting out like fireworks. How it started out the right size when she wore it to games. How it hung so big and baggy at the end.

'Let's go home,' says Lola, suddenly standing up and holding out her hand to me. 'This sucks.' I take it and stand up too, and she puts her arm around me quickly and squeezes.

'Don't you want to see what happens?' asks Maisie.

'The whole thing was probably just some giant prank by Mayor Magnus,' Belle says darkly, picking some ants up on a leaf and throwing them into the lavender bush.

'I don't understand,' I whisper. 'My mum promised she was coming.'

'All those flyers,' says Belle. 'Our strategic five-step campaign. All that meticulous organisation. And for what?'

A cold breeze swirls through the garden, and we shiver. The red Japanese maple sways a little, and a couple more leaves drop to the ground. It's almost bare now. Soon it will be winter. Summer will be even further away.

'Wait!' says Maisie, pointing to the oval. 'Look.'

Someone is running *really* fast across the grass, pumping their arms determinedly. It's –

'JUDY!' we all yell together as she comes into sight.

When she reaches us, she's panting so hard she can't talk.

'Sorry – girls,' she says when she catches her breath, her hands on her knees. 'Freezer – Mikie – cut.'

We look at each other, confused. Mikie cut himself on a freezer? That guy really needs to be more careful.

'Well, you needn't have bothered sprinting over here,' says Belle. 'As you can see, nobody's going to show.'

'The storm,' Judy says, straightening up. 'I had to get a generator for the freezer so the ice-cream wouldn't melt. Because of the power cut,' she adds, looking at our blank faces.

'What power cut?' asks Maisie.

'The storm blew a tree onto the powerlines,' says Judy. 'The whole of Sunnystream has no electricity. That's probably why no-one's here yet. Mikie's just

208

getting his coffee cart. Mr Doozy is putting his dairy stuff into my freezer. Mr Green is packing up all the pies from Sookie La La to bring over here because he's had to shut too.' She grins at us. 'Every single business is going to be closed. Nobody's going to be working. You can expect a big crowd, my friends.'

As usual, Judy is right – within a couple of minutes, people start to flow in from all directions, talking about fridges full of food that might go bad, and meetings being cancelled, and phones that went flat. There's an excitement in the air, an everything-out-of-the-ordinary feeling. Eek! They're here – they're here and they care. If I think about it too much, my heart feels so full that I get teary, so I focus on searching through the crowd to see if I can find Mum.

But not everyone is Full-Heart happy.

'THERE'S NO POWER?' says Belle, sounding kind of shrill. 'What about my microphone?! What are we going to do now? This is all my fault. I should have planned a back-up alternative power source. We should have used some of the bake-sale funds to buy a second-hand generator. I *knew* there was something I was missing. I *knew* that –'

'Shut up about that for a second,' says Maisie. 'How are RexRoy going to play if there's no power?'

Oh. That's not good. And RexRoy aren't even here yet (I think with flat phones and no alarm clocks, there's no way they'd be awake before noon). Lola runs home to fetch them as we watch the crowd build. So many people! How are they going to hear Belle's speech? If Mayor Magnus shows up, he's just going to yell right over the top.

Belle's still going on and on about how stupid she is (um, what? That's ridiculous) when Lola and RexRoy arrive with all their gear. Rishi winks at me, and I practically melt like an ice-cream in a power cut. Then I remember that I'm wearing a dirty unicorn onesie.

'We should have put solar panels on the roof,' Belle raves, 'and installed a mini wind turbine to generate electricity.'

OK, that's insanity, but something she's said is clicking around my mind.

'A generator,' I say slowly. 'Doesn't someone else in town have one of those?' We all think about it for a minute. 'MIKIE!' I say triumphantly. 'He's got one on his coffee cart. I don't know if it's big enough for RexRoy, though ...' We all look at Rishi's giant amps doubtfully.

'I've got another amp – a smaller one,' he says. 'Just for the electric banjo and the mic. It means we couldn't mic the bass or the drums. Does that matter?'

'No!' we say together.

Lola and Maisie go off to find Mikie as Belle suddenly squeals. 'The author of *Sunnystream: A History* is here!' She points through the crowd at an older lady wearing sandals and a jacket made of a bed quilt. 'I think I'm going to faint. MOIRA!' she yells, and dodges through the people. A lot of them are wearing our badges. Judy says she's already run out.

I wish Gracie could see Lemon Tart on the badges. She would have got a real kick out of that. I wish she could see the bright blue door. I stand by myself to the side of the steps, imagining what she'd say. And then I wonder if there'll be a time when I can't remember her voice anymore. I wonder how you hold on to a voice in your mind – if there's anything you can do to keep it there, or if it's like a snowflake, and eventually it'll just melt away so quickly that you won't even be able to say for sure the moment that it left.

You can probably guess that I'm getting the wishing feeling again when two kids our age come up to me. One is a girl, and she is *tall* with long hair like straw and eyes that remind me of hot chocolate that's made from real melted chocolate – not the powdered kind. You can just tell by looking at her that she is kind. The other is a boy, and he only has one eye, the colour of the bluebells that grow by Merry Creek in spring. He's sort of handsome in a neat and responsible way, like he would have been the head boy of his primary school.

'You're from Belle's school!' I say in wonder, feeling as if I'm meeting YouTube stars in real life. 'Matilda. And Pete. I've heard a lot about you guys. Oh – sorry if that's creepy.'

'Totally creepy,' says Pete, and we all laugh, and you know what? Belle was right about his eye – you only notice it for one second and then it's totally normal.

'I can't believe what an amazing job you've done,' Matilda says, but not in a fake, gushy way like the Cloud Town Cougars would. She reaches over and touches my arm. When she looks into my eyes, it's like the Lola Effect but to the power of ten. 'Well done. There must be, like, three hundred people here.'

'Do you know them all?' Pete asks. 'Or are they just randoms?'

I look around and I realise that I DO know them all. I know every single person here. I point them all out to Matilda and Pete, and soon I'm really into giving everyone's little backstory. 'Introduce people with thoughtful details,' my mum used to remind me and Gracie. 'This is Sophia and she's had nits seven times,'

Gracie would say back. (It was actually only six because the seventh time turned out to be chicken pox.)

Mr Morrison, the town building inspector, is here with his wife. Miss Claudine has come from Cloud Town. Coach Jack is deep in conversation with Mr and Mrs Zhang, but I can't tell from here how that's going. Judy is handing out free ice-creams, so the Eco Worriers are hanging out nearby, and Mr and Mrs Green from Sookie La La are giving away slices of peach pie. Mr Doozy from Buck's and Ms Sadlier, our year four teacher, and the whole of my mum's real-estate networking group are here.

Francine and Punk Sherman are walking round hand in hand.

'I don't know if I'm ready to meet my girlfriend's mum,' Pete says in a sort of panic, flattening down his hair, and he looks so scared that Matilda and I laugh again.

'Soph!' Maisie calls, and I turn around to see that the others are already on the verandah with Mikie. And – I kid you not! – Pony Soprano is there too. I need to get up there.

'Good luck!' say Matilda and Pete.

'Catch you after,' I reply as I climb the steps, and I really hope I do.

We're standing on the verandah, right at the front. Belle Brodie and Lola Powell and Maisie Zhang and Pony Soprano and me. The band is squished in behind us, ready to play, but the crowd is still chattering expectantly, waiting to see if Mayor Magnus is going to show up.

'This is awkward,' says Lola, and we all kind of giggle.

I wish I'd had time to put on proper clothes and wasn't standing in front of everyone in this unicorn onesie.

Pony Soprano harrumphs out his nostrils. The crowd laughs. And then they go completely quiet, like the whole of Sunnystream is holding its breath.

At half past ten, a bus pulls up. Out of it spill a whole heap of guys, maybe forty of them, wearing yellow hard hats and fluoro orange vests. They look like just the kind of gang you'd want to have around if you were ripping down a building. They stand to the side of the crowd, near the front. They're kind of intimidating. Suddenly it all feels too real. My tummy goes all tight.

Rishi comes over and puts his arm around my shoulder. It's warm and strong, and for a moment, I want to lean my cheek against his chest. 'Shall we start playing?' he asks.

I feel a lump in my throat. Lola has tears in her eyes. Maisie is standing so still. I swallow. I try to sound calm, like it's no big deal. 'Yes please, Rishi,' I say. 'That would be awesome.'

Rishi goes back and sits on his drum stool. He whacks his drumsticks together three times and the band begins to play. The song is so catchy that by the last chorus, even Moira is singing along.

'*Muscle Tower versus PEOPLE POWER!*'

At the end people go *crazy*. They don't stop cheering until something starts beeping super loud.

'Has the generator malfunctioned?' Belle asks.

But it's not the speakers. It's Mayor Magnus, riding across the oval in another giant bulldozer, waving. Even from here I can see that he's wearing his purple sparkly cape. Next to him is Bart Strabonsky and he's dressed as a cowboy. They've both got those headset microphones that pop stars wear when they're singing live in concert. Oh brother.

CHAPTER 20

As soon as the crowd works out what's happening, they boo those bozos. But Mayor Magnus can't get enough of the attention. He parks his bulldozer next to the other bulldozer, opens the door and waves again, blowing kisses, his honey-blond hair waving in the breeze. The booing gets even louder. He and Bart Strabonsky climb down and squeeze onto the verandah next to us. Jules doesn't even have time to unplug his banjo; Mayor Magnus just kind of bumps RexRoy down the clubhouse stairs.

'Show's over, folks!' The crowd boos again as Mayor Magnus yells, 'KABOOM!'

That must have been a cue, because at that second

the guys in hard hats break out of their bunch and form a line between the clubhouse and the front of the crowd, their backs to the verandah, their arms crossed over their chests.

'Listen up, Sunnystream,' yells Mayor Magnus. 'Do not believe the lies that were published in the *Sunnystream Gazette*. The Shark Tank is a VERY safe building. It's a very BIG building. And as we all know, bigger is better! Which is why this little bitty cubbyhouse has to go. It's being knocked over to make way for … the Muscle Tower! An apartment block like you have never seen. Complete with an aquarium and its own … real life … fully functioning … SUBMARINE!'

People look at each other like, 'Is this guy for real? Why the fudge would you put a real-life submarine in a fish tank?'

But then his voice gets more menacing. He glares at the crowd so hard that his eyebrows almost cross. 'This terrific new project will bring in money and jobs and great new opportunities. SO! It's very clear to me that anyone who's against the Muscle Tower wants Sunnystream to *suffer*.'

What?! That actually makes zero sense. Who loves Sunnystream more than Belle and Maisie and Lola and me? But right then everyone goes quiet, as if they're possibly half-convinced that Mayor Magnus might be right.

Two men in hard hats stride over to the bulldozers and jump up into the drivers' seats. They start the engines. The rest of the men in hard hats link arms. And then slowly, slowly they start moving their line forward, pushing the crowd back, away from the clubhouse. I can see Matilda and Pete trying to hold their ground, but they're swept up in the wave of people inching backwards. Everyone is. I think I'm going to spew.

Belle jumps up and down on the verandah, waving her arms to get people's attention. 'STOP! Hey! Listen here!'

But nobody notices – they're just trying not to fall over as they're all forced back. After everything we've done and all that we've fought for, we're not going to get our say after all.

That's when Rishi ducks under the arms of the hard-hat guys and jumps back up the stairs. He strums Jules's electric banjo as loud as he can. The sound is DEAFENING, and the hard-hat men turn around to see what made it. A couple let go of each other to cover their ears. The crowd stops moving.

Belle grabs the microphone and holds it just the right distance away from her mouth so that her voice comes out clear and strong. (She practised this for her TED Talk – maybe even for ten thousand hours.) She's holding her notebook open with her other hand, not that she needs it. She's memorised the whole speech.

'Good morning, Sunnystream! Let me cut to the chase. You can believe Mayor Magnus's empty promises,' she says smoothly. 'You can trust someone who has lied to us and put our lives in danger. Or you can look around at this beautiful building. You can look into your past and your family history, and I guarantee, you'll find this clubhouse there, front and centre.' (Dramatic pause.) 'It's not just a building. It's a time capsule for our whole town. It's a place for us to come together. And we want to make it into a home again for us all. You'll see that it's been returned to its former glory, and it's ready to host all of Sunnystream's most cherished events once more. With our families, we can …'

She stops. And then the weirdest thing happens. She's got pages and pages more of her speech to recite, but Belle starts to cry. We're so shocked that we all just kind of freeze. But that's nothing compared to what comes next.

She looks up at Mayor Magnus – like, *really* looks at him. 'Dad,' she says through her tears. 'Please?'

DAD? What the fudge?! Me and Maisie and Lola turn to each other like, 'WHAT?!' I don't think I have ever been so surprised.

But it all makes sense. I remember how Mayor Magnus's face crumpled when we didn't want to stay and look at his fish tank. I remember how his secretary let Belle into his office. What Belle said about wishing she didn't know who her dad was when we were eating marshmallows that night at the clubhouse. How they glare the same, like their eyebrows almost cross. Their hair, the same kind of honey blonde. How much they both like to speak in public – how they're each so good at it in their own way. It all makes so much sense that I feel stupid for not putting it together before. My mind is literally blown.

Now Mayor Magnus is looking at Belle, really looking at her. He's looking at her like I caught my dad looking at Gracie once, when she was bundled on the sofa with Lemon Tart. Like he was longing for something. It must have been so hard for him, my dad. And for the first time, I start to understand why he had to move away. Then Mayor Magnus moves towards Belle, like he might be going to hug her.

But Belle turns her back. She drops the microphone and buries her head in her hands and starts crying again. Maisie and I look at each other. Mayor Magnus just stands there awkwardly. Jeepers. He looks sad. I put my arm around Belle, but she doesn't lean into me, and I wonder if I've done the right thing.

Thankfully, Tally jumps up onto the verandah and picks up the microphone, which is sort of hard because she's holding a giant stack of paper, thicker than a dictionary. She's wearing a pleated hot-pink skirt that touches the floor and a silver sequined headscarf that glitters in the sun. Maisie edges over to her and takes the pile of paper so she doesn't have to hold it while she talks.

'Mayor Magnus, here's a petition,' she says. 'Signatures from …' She pauses dramatically. 'A *quarter of a million* people all over the world who think that Corner Park Clubhouse should be saved.'

The crowd gasps.

Mayor Magnus swallows and scoffs. 'That's just loons on the internet. You think this means anything in the real world, girly?'

'Well, most of them have donated to our crowd-funding campaign, too,' Tally says coolly. 'A dollar each. There's enough money to keep this place running for a decade. Is that real enough for you?'

If there's one thing Mayor Magnus responds to, it's money. Now he's starting to look uncomfortable. He looks across at Belle and his shoulders slump.

That's when Bart Strabonsky steps forward, his chest puffed up, and lifts off his hat. He waves it at us – Belle and Lola and Maisie and me. '*YOU*. You broke into council property. You operated a business here without a proper licence. You defaced it with mindless, ugly graffiti. Terrible graffiti.'

Wait a minute – is he talking about *kintsugi?!*

'You broke the LAW. You're a gang of delinquent tweens. And you want to trust these criminals?' he asks, turning to the crowd.

It's awkward because technically he's right. Well, apart from the delinquent teenagers part. What we've done probably isn't legal. But does that mean it's wrong? *Are* we criminals?

There's a stunned kind of silence. Slowly, Bart Strabonsky starts to smirk. I want to barf into his stupid tall hat. But then he gets carried away. 'You bunch of meddling little twits! You disgusting feral rats. You nut-job slimeballs! You –'

'Um, excuse me?' calls someone in the middle of the crowd. 'Have some respect. You're talking to children.

You're talking to some very clever, very compassionate, very responsible children.'

It's Coach Jack! His hair is out of the man bun and it's long and glinty-blond, like a lion's mane. I bet Lola is digging this. And yes, what he's saying is good too.

'We could all learn a lot from this gang,' he continues. '*You* could learn a lot from them.'

'Who is this guy – some kind of hippy with pretty girl's hair?' says Bart Strabonsky viciously. I can feel Belle flinch because he's using 'girl' as a derogatory term. NOT cool.

'What a joke,' Bart continues. 'You, sir, are a joke. This whole dinky little clubhouse is a joke. It's nothing. *You're* nothing.'

'He is NOT nothing,' I say loudly, stepping forward. 'And this isn't just a clubhouse.' Whoa – I am kind of trembling now with rage and nerves but also some weird kind of excitement, like something inside me is boiling. It's like debating but on steroids. The whole town is looking at me. And this time, nobody can look away.

CHAPTER 21

'Until the Shark Tank came along, people made memories here,' I say. 'It's where kids learned how to live good lives,' I say, thinking of Girl Guides and storytime and how hard Gracie practised for the Sunny Stream of Talent.

I look out at all the people – so many people! – and I wonder if my mum is even here, or if she's been called away for another house, another sale. 'Mr Morrison got married in the clubhouse fifty years ago,' I continue, 'because he met his wife at the dances they used to hold here for young people. The first women to get the vote in Sunnystream cast their ballots here. It's where the whole of Sunnystream came to watch man walk on the moon. On the walls inside are the names of everyone from our community who ever fought in a war.'

Belle gives me a huge thumbs-up for remembering this part of *Sunnystream: A History*.

I take a deep breath. 'And when my twin, Gracie, died, after the funeral we came here. Everyone we knew came here. People told stories about her. And when I'm here, for a little while I don't feel like she's gone.' I wiggle my toes inside my ugg boots and I make myself keep going. 'We might not have used it much lately, but sometimes you just need reminding how … how precious something is. Sometimes you need to almost lose it to find your way back again.'

I can feel something pass through the crowd like wind in a wheat field. Like a gentle breeze of memories. Everyone in town knew Gracie, and they loved her. Maybe you think I'm just saying that because she's not here anymore, but it's true. She had these big mad black curls that sprang out from her head like they were jumping. She had cool glasses that made her look smart. Gracie *was* smart. Last year she only got one question wrong in the entire Maths Olympiad. She even beat Isaac J, an all-round genius who does Gifted and Talented oboe classes and has his own Sudoku website.

She taught herself to play the trumpet – no lessons or anything. She played it every Anzac Day at the Sunnystream dawn service. When she was Head Girl of Sunnystream Primary, she wrote a poem about time to read at the year six graduation party, and literally zero people could believe it was made up by a kid. She read it from her wheelchair and it took her ages, but when she got to the end, the clapping went on forever. Nobody wanted to stop, and maybe secretly we were all thinking that if we just kept clapping, Gracie would keep on living.

And she was so kind. I bet you're thinking I'm only saying that because of what happened, but it's true. Gracie could always make people feel better – kids who'd wet their pants in assembly or come last in a swimming race. At Christmas time, she made jars of brownie mix for the teachers who nobody would get presents for, so that all they had to do was add in the eggs and bake them. When Grandma Jean was in Sunny Heights, the nursing home, it was Gracie who got us all to go there and sing rounds and plant the tulip patch. And sometimes I think … I think she was going to have a really good life. Better than mine was ever going to be. But I'm here. And she's not.

'I bet everyone in Sunnystream has their own special

memory of the clubhouse,' I say. 'And we can start making them again – right from today. Isn't that worth more than money? Isn't that better than an apartment building? Isn't that worth saving?'

Bart Strabonsky is silent for a moment.

Mayor Magnus is too, which is probably a first. Eventually he says, 'Girly, your sister died. I get it. But it takes people to run a public building and to organise all those silly little town events. You think Bart and I have time for that?'

I think back to them playing Snap in his office, and you know what? I think they probably do.

'That's why we're here,' says Lola. 'We've totally got this.'

Bart Strabonsky sniggers. 'You think we're going to trust a public building to a bunch of ten-year-olds? Outrageous.'

'We're twelve,' Maisie says flatly. 'Almost thirteen. And we could do it with our eyes closed.'

'There's, ahh, there's some safety rules that you won't know about –' Mayor Magnus begins.

'Yeah, like the safety regulations you followed when you built the Shark Tank?' calls Judy, jutting out her chin.

There's a murmur in the crowd and I hear a few

people saying things like, 'Yes – exactly!' and 'I agree!

'As the town's building inspector, I'm happy to keep an eye on the place,' calls Mr Morrison from the front row. 'From a safety perspective.'

'You could supervise the planned working bees,' says Belle. 'I've scheduled them in monthly. We've already built a website for the bookings – well, Maisie did. She's a coding genius.'

Maisie blushes and I know she'd be hating this. I look out and spot her parents. They are grinning proudly.

Mayor Magnus is pouting now, like a giant baby. 'What about – what about – what about setting up for all the events? Events need chairs. LOTS of chairs. How's a bunch of little girls going to do that?'

'The band boys and I can help,' says Rishi, and they all nod enthusiastically. 'But these girls are actually pretty strong.'

'We won't be paying you,' spits Bart Strabonsky.

'Dude, not everything's about money,' says Rishi, and I get the tummy love feeling even stronger than before.

'I'll be around the place,' calls Mikie. 'With my cart. Keeping an eye on it.'

'And I'll be keeping an eye on *him*,' calls Judy.

Everyone laughs, but not in a mean way. Everyone

knows how clumsy Mikie is. It's one of the things we all love about him.

'Speaking of money,' says Belle. Her eyes are still red but at least she has her voice back. 'This will generate quite a bit of money for the town – people hiring out the clubhouse and all. Do you gentlemen have any objections to *that*?' She closes her notebook with a satisfied snap.

Mayor Magnus is glaring so hard, I think his eyebrows are crossing over one another. He looks like a kid who just lost at Monopoly. Bart Strabonsky is prancing from foot to foot and punching the bottom of his cowboy hat. Is this it? Have we won?!

From the crowd, I hear a voice ring out – one I've known so well for so long. It's Patrick. 'Cor-ner PARK, Cor-ner PARK.'

Judy joins him, and Rishi and RexRoy, and I do too. I don't know if I've ever yelled so hard – not even for Maisie when she finished her Level 9 floor routine by doing jazz hands and won a silver medal.

'COR-NER PARK! COR-NER PARK!' The crowd is so loud, I can feel it like a buzz through my body – like we're standing on a verandah made of bees. I can see Matilda and Pete screaming it too, and then I see her – my mum. Tears are streaming down her face as she chants with the crowd. She's here – she's actually here, and not at some emergency work meeting. Not showing people around a house on Tea Cake Crescent. And wait … Is that –?

But I can't be sure, because right then Lola grabs my hand, and I grab Maisie's, and she grabs Belle's. We turn and look at each other, our faces shining. Then we raise our hands together, and the whole crowd roars.

The guys with the hard hats drop arms and turn to look at Mayor Magnus, as if to say, 'Well?' And suddenly everyone's quiet again, waiting for what he's going to say.

'FINE!' yells Mayor Magnus, ripping off his cape and throwing it onto the ground. 'I didn't even want to pull down the stupid clubhouse anyway.'

Pony Soprano trots over and snaps the cape up in his mouth and starts chewing. Everyone starts laughing, and Bart Strabonsky tries to yank Mayor Magnus off-stage to stop him embarrassing himself. (Might be a bit too late for that, buddy.) They're about to get into an actual fistfight when Mikie pushes through the crowd and climbs the steps so he's standing next to Lola, who is *beaming*, by the way. She grabs the microphone from me and taps it to get people's attention. Then she passes it to Mikie.

'Mayor Magnus, does the clubhouse do weddings?' Mikie asks.

Those doofuses stop scuffling for a second. 'There's a fee,' Mayor Magnus pants, tired from wrestling. 'A HUGE fee.'

Belle glares at him so hard her eyebrows *definitely* cross. She crosses her arms too. 'Sunnystream Council Regulations state that the fee for weddings in Corner Park is eighty dollars,' she says. 'It's on your website. The clubhouse is in this park and is not listed separately.' She turns back to Mikie. 'So yes, we do weddings. Eighty bucks and it's yours.'

Mikie wipes his hands on his pants. And then he actually gets down on one knee and faces out into the crowd. Everyone gasps. I told you this was better than TV.

'Judy,' he says. 'Will you do me the honour of being my wife?'

And if you think that was crazy, you will literally not believe what happens next. As Judy flies up onto the verandah to kiss him and everyone is going crazy – whooping and throwing things in the air – someone else jumps up the stairs. Someone with curls that spring out from his head, grey ones, and the kindest blue eyes in the world.

'Dad!' I breathe.

'Hope you don't mind if I copy your idea,' Dad says to Mikie, and the whole town laughs. He tries to get down on one knee, but he's kind of old, and maybe not as bendy as Mikie nowadays. It takes him ages and the crowd laughs again. OMG, what is happening here?! I'm sort of embarrassed and sort of out of my mind with happiness to see him again. I guess I'm conflicted, or at least that's what Belle would say.

I think of him and Mum sitting on the steps in bare feet on a warm breezy night before I was even here. How much Gracie loved that story on long car rides home.

'Julie,' Dad says to my mum when the crowd hushes down. 'Will you marry me … again?'

CHAPTER 22

As everyone pours into the clubhouse to see what we've done, Dad wraps me in a hug that goes on forever. To Tuesday and back, as Gracie would say. We might as well be in space, on a tiny Swedish island, in a crystal-filled cave – even though we're in the middle of the crowd, it's like we're the only two people in the world. I can feel his tears dripping down, cool on my hair. 'Oh, Pickle,' he whispers.

When we let each other go, Mum comes up and grabs me tight. You can tell she does bootcamp by those arm muscles. 'Grace would be so proud of you,' she whispers. '*I'm* proud.'

She smells so familiar, like laundry and almond

hand cream. As she lets me go, I look up into her face. She seems so much older than I remember and it gives me a little shock. She's not a robot, I want to tell Gracie. She's just a human. For real.

'I know I've been working too much these last few months,' she says as we go down the steps, Dad's arm around her shoulder, her arm around mine. 'It's just that … When I'm working … when I'm working …' She looks down at her rings, twisting one of them with her thumb, like she's nervous.

'When you're working, you don't have to remember all the time,' I say to them both. 'I get it.'

Mum nods. 'It's not real. Not yet. It doesn't seem unlikely to me that she could still walk through a doorway. Appear from behind a bush. If I just keep working, that's still a possibility.'

But it's not a real possibility. She knows that, and I know that, and Dad knows that.

'It was wrong of me to run away,' he says. 'And I'm sorry. I was just …'

His voice trails off. But I know what he is trying to say. 'You were just lost,' I finish, 'because it was always Gracie who showed us the way.' We look at each other, sort of half gobsmacked, because, though no-one's ever said that before, it's suddenly so obvious.

'But, Dad?' I say eventually. 'She's not here, but she's not gone. Not really.'

Mum grips Dad's hand, and he strokes her thumb with his big thumb. I must have seen him do that a million times in my life. A squillion.

'You're together,' I say in wonder.

'We were never apart,' says Mum. 'Not … not really. I've been trying to tell you. But you didn't seem to want to listen.'

I think of all the times when I blocked my ears and said LA LA LA. I wonder what else I missed because I wasn't ready to hear. But I am now.

Out of the corner of my eye, I see Maisie and Lola and Belle by the stegosaurus slide, waving at me to come over.

'Go on, sweetheart,' Mum says. 'See you at home.'

I start to run, but then I turn back to my parents. 'Wait – you guys should go and look at the red Japanese maple. There's something on the trunk you might like to see.'

And then I sprint over to my friends. It's only twenty steps away, but I can't get there fast enough.

I don't know if I can actually describe how intense our group hug is, so I'll leave it to your imagination, but make sure you add in the part where we're jumping up and down so much that we topple over into the woodchips at the bottom of the slide and end up picking them out of each other's hair like baboons do. While we're doing that, we debrief on everything that just happened. Belle's dad being Mayor Magnus. My dad coming back to Sunnystream. And of course, saving the clubhouse, AKA VICTORY!

'We saved you, Corner Park Clubhouse,' Lola yells at the pretty white building – our own tiny Hogwarts. And I swear, it's like the building winks a thank-you back.

'I don't mean to be a killjoy,' says Maisie later on, when we're sitting at our favourite picnic table, drinking hot chocolates. Turns out they're not too babyish after all. 'But if we're all in different places during term time, how are we *actually* going to make this work? How are we going to keep the clubhouse going, I mean.'

I think Belle's going to say 'organisation' or 'planning' or 'scheduling' or 'a shared electronic calendar'. But she doesn't.

'*This* is what's going to make it work,' she says simply. 'Us. We love each other too much to let it slip away.'

'Gracie …' I say. I clear my throat and try again. 'Gracie always used to say there was nothing the four of us couldn't do.' The others are looking at me and smiling – sort of sad smiles, but still smiles. I guess I haven't said her name to them since she died.

Gracie didn't hang out with us heaps but she really liked these guys. She thought Belle was so funny in her crazy, nerdy, genius way. She thought Lola was cool, of course (who doesn't?), but she wondered what would happen as we grew up – if she'd become one of those popular girls who you couldn't quite trust with your secrets. She liked how Maisie doesn't care what anyone thinks, she just is who she is.

You might think it's weird that Gracie wasn't in our group, because we were twins and all, but it wasn't. It's just that she had Patrick, and they did everything together. Suddenly, so much about Gracie is pouring into my mind. She and Patrick in their baseball uniforms, throwing the ball back and forth as they walked up our street. Gracie up on Dad's back at a Father's Day picnic race, wearing his sunglasses over her real glasses. Gracie on the flying fox before she was sick, kicking her legs as she flew through the purple summer sky.

'Gracie wasn't a jealous person,' I say to the others.

'But she was jealous of our friendship. She never said that out loud. But after she died, I read her diary. Do you think that's bad?' I've worried about this heaps, to be honest.

'No,' they all say together, and they look like they mean it.

'I would have, for sure,' says Maisie.

'That is perfectly natural human behaviour,' says Belle.

'I would have tried to read it the second I found out about it,' says Lola.

I laugh. I'm super relieved. It feels so good to talk about Gracie. Like she's real, and not this weird mix between that ghost from Harry Potter that haunts the bathrooms and a cement bag on my back. 'You want to know something else? I'm sort of mad at her for dying. But at the same time … At the same time …' I stop, because it's almost too big to say. I wipe my eyes with my palms. Maybe it's too big *not* to say. Maybe I'll have to say it one day, someday, and this is that day, and these are the people to hear it.

I close my eyes. I think about the bruises on Gracie's arms from all the needles and drips. How even when she wanted to wrestle on the TV-room sofa, I would be thinking about not touching them too hard. I think about how she knew that's what I was thinking, and it made her wrestle harder.

I think about the last day of Gracie's life, when she pushed Lemon Tart right off the bed, a big angry push. When I picked Lemon Tart up from the carpet, she was trembling. She wouldn't stop – not for hours. I held her and held her but she just kept shaking. Maisie came over and took her that day because I couldn't hold her anymore. She's kept her ever since. But I think now I might be ready to take her back.

I take a deep breath and look down at my hands. 'At the same time I'm glad Gracie's not sick anymore. I'm glad that it's over. And I'm worried that makes me a terrible person. But it's just how I feel. Sort of relieved. Because it was hard to watch her be so brave. And also, when she was sick I sort of … disappeared.'

I look up and see that Lola is crying. Twice in one week – this is an actual record. 'You're not a terrible person,' she says. 'You're so sweet and kind. I don't know why, of all the people in the world, this had to happen to you.'

Maisie nods. 'It's not fair. That's what I just keep thinking. It's so not fair.'

'I know you find it hard to talk about it. But I just want you to know that we're here for you,' says Belle.

'*A pain shared is half the pain. A pleasure shared is twice the pleasure.*'

'Is that Shakespeare again?' Maisie asks.

'A Swedish proverb,' says Belle.

'I'm so putting that on my Instagram,' says Lola, wiping her tears and standing up. 'But not right now.' She nods to the others and holds out her hand to me. I link arms and she squeezes mine in tight next to her body. 'I want to show you something. Close your eyes.'

Luckily we don't have to go far because it's tricky, walking through the darkness. Twice I almost trip, but Lola catches me. I don't think the others are with us. It feels as if we're somewhere a bit quieter when she says, 'Now open them.'

We are round the side of the clubhouse with the eucalyptus trees – at the back, where there's a little clearing. In the crisp sunlight, the white wall is glowing golden. And there's something painted on the side of the building. Like a giant black-and-white photograph. Lola's arm is still in mine, but I can feel her whole body tense up, waiting.

I don't say anything. I can't say anything.

I just look and look.

'Is it OK?' she whispers.

I shake my arm free and sit down on the ground, hugging my knees.

'I never want to leave here,' I say eventually. 'I'm never going to.'

'Really?' she says. 'Oh phew.' She sounds so relieved.

'Lola,' I say. 'It's perfect. When did you – how?'

She looks down and proud-smiles. 'Come back when you're ready,' she says, and starts walking back to the others.

There, on the wall, is Gracie – the top half of her, anyway. There's her face, round with the dimple I always wished was mine. There are the ringlets that jumped from her head, like coils of electricity. Her glasses with their flecked frames, the colour of Coke when you hold it to the sun in a glass. And there are her eyes, happy in a cheeky way. 'Come on,' they are saying. 'Let's go!'

'Gracie,' I whisper with wonder. 'Gracie, I miss you.'

As I gaze up at her, I can hear her voice, husky like it was when she'd stayed up late reading and dragged herself out of bed for Saturday-morning waffles.

'Me too,' she says. 'I'm sorry I'm gone. I'm sorry I left you.'

'That's OK,' I say. 'It's getting better.'

And for the first time, I think I really mean it.

When it's too cold to sit there any longer, I stand up. As I brush grass off my legs, something on the clubhouse wall catches my eye. I go closer so I can see it properly.

On Gracie's shirt, right in the middle, there's a heart. Running through it are little cracks of gold, like tiny rivers. They flash as they catch the last glow of sunset. And there's something else in the bottom right corner. It's a gold plaque, new and shiny.

The Grace Hargraves Memorial Clubhouse, it says.

I turn around and they're behind me, waiting – Belle Brodie, Lola Powell and Maisie Zhang. And maybe Grace Hargraves is too. I get the Full Heart feeling again.

And this time the words don't catch in my throat. They just tumble right on out in a string, and I say, 'Guys! Best friends forever?'

'Literally,' says Lola.

'Obviously,' says Belle.

Through the twilight, I can see Maisie smile. 'Yeah,' she says. 'Forever.'

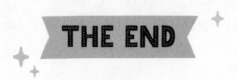

THE END

and this is the wonder that's keeping the stars apart

i carry your heart(i carry it in my heart)

— e.e. cummings

Seven Questions

1. Ever told a lie to this group?
   Once I faked a stomach ache because I knew I had to get up early for gym. Also my Chinese name doesn't mean 'cute bean shoot'. Sorry, guys!

2. What do you want to be when you grow up?
   Assassin. Jokes — Olympic-champion gymnast.

3. Who is your crush?
   NOT Coach Jack, and I don't care what you say, Lola, it's true.

4. Serve ice-cream at Judy's in the nude OR wet your pants at the Anzac Service?
   Ice-cream.

5. Grass seeds in your undies or kissing Bart Strabonsky (tongue)?
   Grass seeds. PS. GROSS.

6. Person I like the most here:
   Soph, my BFF.

7. The worst thing that ever happened:
   When Gracie got sick and I couldn't make it better.

1. Ever told a lie to this group?
   I value honesty above all else.
2. What do you want to be when you grow up?
   Environmental activist and human rights lawyer.
3. Who is your crush?
   My current boyfriend.
4. Serve ice-cream at Judy's in the nude OR wet your pants at the Anzac Service?
   Wet pants, though I respect the right to express body confidence in all forms.
5. Grass seeds in your undies or kissing Bart Strabonsky (tongue)?
   Grass seeds. (Whoever thought of this is a monster.)
6. Person I like the most here:
   Sophia
7. The worst thing that ever happened:
   The day Gracie's hair fell out.

1. Ever told a lie to this group?
   Yep, last week. Not saying what, tho ☺
2. What do you want to be when you grow up?
   Painter
3. Who is your crush?
   Jules from RexRoy, Achok from school,
   Coach Jack (obvs), Ben (who works at
   Buck's), the guy who took us on a tour
   of the Refuse and Recycling Plant at
   Willowbank in year five.
4. Serve ice-cream at Judy's in the nude OR
   wet your pants at the Anzac Service?
   Judy's. Nothing wrong with nude!
5. Grass seeds in your undies or kissing
   Bart Strabonsky (tongue)?
   Can my eyes be closed? If yes, kissing.
   Actually, kissing anyway.
6. Person I like the most here:
   Soph
7. The worst thing that ever happened:
   Gracie's funeral ☹

Quote Board

'and this is the wonder that's
keeping the stars apart

i carry your heart(i carry it
in my heart)'

– e.e. cummings, '[i carry your heart
with me(i carry it in]', *Complete
Poems: 1904–1962* (Liveright
Publishing Corporation, 1991)

'Time is how you spend your
love.'

– Nick Laird, 'The Last Saturday in
Ulster', *To a Fault* (Faber, 2005)

'Kites rise highest against
the wind, not with it.'

Adapted from: 'Kites rise against,
and not with, the wind.'
– John Neal (1793–1876);
commonly attributed to Winston
Churchill

'There is no love; there are
only proofs of love.'

– Pierre Reverdy (1889–1960)

'If you're going through hell,
keep going.'

– commonly attributed to
Winston Churchill

'To describe how I miss you
isn't possible. It would be
like blue trying to describe
the ocean.'

Adapted from: 'To convey in any
existing language how I miss you
isn't possible. It would be like blue
trying to describe the ocean.'
– Mary-Louise Parker, *Dear Mr. You*
(Scribner, 2015)

CORNER PARK CLUBHOUSE

Book 2 – coming soon!

THE SECRET LIFE OF LOLA

It's the winter holidays, and Lola and her best friends, Belle, Maisie and Sophia, are in charge of putting together a Sunnystream musical for a huge competition!

But how can the show go on when their Cloud Town rivals are psyching them out, Pony Soprano is too busy to rehearse, and Lola's got a dark secret that's giving her a bad case of painter's block?

About the author

Davina Bell is an award-winning writer for young readers of many ages. She writes picture books (including *All the Ways to be Smart* and *Under the Love Umbrella*), junior fiction (*Lemonade Jones*) and middle-grade fiction (the Corner Park Clubhouse series and the *Alice* books in the Our Australian Girl series). Davina wishes she were a Lola but is probably more of a Soph with a splash of Belle. Originally from Western Australia, she now lives in Melbourne, where she works as a children's book editor.